JAMES PRINTER

A Novel of Rebellion

by Paul Samuel Jacobs

SCHOLASTIC PRESS • NEW YORK

LIBRARY OF CONGRESS CATALOGING-IN-PUBLICATION DATA

Jacobs, Paul Samuel.
James Printer : a novel of rebellion / by Paul Samuel Jacobs.
p.   cm.
Summary: Although he has lived and worked as a printer's apprentice
with the Green family in Cambridge, Massachusetts, for many years,
James, a Nipmuck Indian, finds himself caught up in the events that
lead to a horrible war.

ISBN 0-590-16381-7
1. King Philip's War, 1675–1676 — Juvenile fiction. [1. King Philip's War,
1675–1676 — Fiction. 2. Printer, James — Fiction.
3. Indians of North America — Massachusetts — Fiction.
4. Massachusetts — History — Colonial period, ca. 1600–1775 — Fiction.
5. Printers — Fiction.]   I. Title.
PZ7.J15253Jam   1997   96-25937
[Fic] — dc20   CIP   AC
12 11 10 9 8 7 6 5 4 3 2 1   7 8 9/9 0 1 2/0

Printed in the U.S.A.
First printing, May 1997

Title page illustration by Mark Summers
Book design by Marijka Kostiw

To Nancy Marlene Jacobs

More than twenty-five years ago and newly married, we visited the Fruitlands Museum in Harvard, Massachusetts, where I taught school. That's when we first heard of James Printer and thought of writing a book about him. Without Nancy's research and patience, love and friendship, this work would not have been possible.

CHAPTER ONE

AWAKENING DAY

I REMEMBER THE DAY I FIRST SAW KING
Philip.

My half-brother, Sam, rousted me from bed
long before the sun began its climb across the
sky. "Make quick," he said in his usual morning
voice, which was loud and grating. "Work's
waiting to be done."

Still, on this day, I left my warm bed without
either complaint or delay. I washed my face by
the thin light of a sputtering candle and smiled

to myself in the little mirror above the basin. There I was, the same Bartholomew Green I had been before. The same clump of hair stood up stubbornly on my head, refusing to bend before my brush. The same gray eyes, now cleared of sleep, blinked back at me. The same small ears stuck out from my head just a little too much.

Yet all was to be different this day. An awakening day, I call it, when everything had to be noticed.

I raced downstairs, skipping steps in my haste. My brother already sat in the kitchen glumly eating his breakfast. He was almost twenty years my senior, the hair upon his head already wispy, and his face grown tired, soft around the chin and puffy about the eyes.

"Never have I seen you move so quick," he said. "Going somewhere this day?"

"We're going to Boston," said my cousin Annie, who sat across the table. She squinted up at me from her bowl, her spoon gripped in her hand. "Aren't we, Bartholomew?"

Annie was as overjoyed as my older brother was gloomy. He after all was to stay behind in Cambridge, toiling with my father in our print shop. "There is work to be done in Boston, do not forget that," Sam reminded her.

She ignored him, while eating hurriedly. I admired the way her hunger outraced even mine, as if no amount of mush mixed with goat's milk and dried currants could ever satisfy her. Her face was dusted with freckles from working with my mother in the garden, and there was a golden streak in her long brown hair.

"I wonder what ships will be in the harbor," she said. "And what fine persons we shall see. I hear that the ladies wear lace in Boston, and all the men wear capes and collars of fur."

My mother put my bowl before me, just as my father came to take his seat at the table. He seemed old to me this morning. I could see the gray in the stubble of his beard.

"Is it safe for the children to go," my mother asked him, "at such a time as this?" Safe? I wondered what she meant. This was not a season of blizzards or hurricanoes, and the road to Boston was an easy one in all but the worst of weather.

My father waved away her fears. "Of course, Mistress Green, it is safe for them to go. All this talk of uprisings is foolish prattle. A little argument between a farmer and an Indian boy is not a call to arms."

I had not heard any talk of uprisings before this or of a quarrel between a farmer and an Indian. I looked to my mother and saw the shadows of worry about her deep-set eyes, but she said nothing.

I was eleven in that year of 1675, on a day when my eyes were truly open. An awakening day, as I have said. My cousin and I were to go to Boston with James, the apprentice printer in my father's shop.

You might have heard of my father, Master Samuel Green, the printer who ran the presses at Harvard College in Cambridge town. People said that he was the finest printer in the New England colonies and as good as any who worked in London. And I, a lump of clay barely formed into the shape of a man, was the devil in his shop. The printer's devil, I mean—the one expected to sweep and scrub, and run for this or bend for that, and set things right when type was spilled or bent or broken.

Oh, I hated the work, as all boys, before and since, do hate the little jobs that are theirs to do. But even so, I was proud to call myself a printer's devil and work alongside my father and my half-brother, Sam, and especially the apprentice James.

Maybe you have heard of James, too. He became famous in his time, before this tale of mine is done. He shared in King Philip's fame. But not just yet on that spring morning, when James walked into our kitchen before the sky gave up the last stars to a fiery dawn. You could tell right away that he was not like the others. He was taller by far than my father or brother. His hair and his eyes were black as charcoal. He was handsome, I thought, even though his face had been scarred by the smallpox.

He was an Indian, but I did not think of him so. If you closed your eyes and heard him speak, you would not have known it. He talked like any Englishman, but much faster. His words raced from him in a wild gallop, like a horse without a rider.

"I have the cart loaded, Master Green," he said, "all the books stacked as snugly as bricks in a wall. Such a pretty volume, the lines as true as a schoolmaster's ruler. The bookseller will not have them long, before they are sold."

How cheerful he was, so early in the morning. But was there ever a time when he was not cheerful? I knew him all of my life, but I had never seen him either sad or angry. Until this spring day he seemed to be a man without fears or worries.

"To Boston, we will journey," he said, as if we were traveling to a far-off land. In truth, it was a trip of just a few hours each way, across the river Charles. But for me and my cousin Annie Clark, it might have been a journey over the sea, to Spain or Africa, to the West Indies or the Virginia colony.

I sat high atop our wagon, between James and Annie. I was not a quiet boy. It only seemed so between the two of them. They both chattered as we moved along. No person or house, no flowering plant or grazing animal, could we pass without a comment.

Annie was the daughter of my mother's brother, Robert Clark, newly arrived from England with his small family. They were to stay by us only briefly before they moved to the town of Deerfield, far to the west. But one day over supper, my mother announced to all that my cousin Annie was to stay behind.

"My brother thinks that Deerfield is too new, just yet," my mother announced. "Robert does not believe it right for a young girl to live like a savage in the wilderness. So Annie must stay with us until a proper house is built. When all is settled he will come for her, and not before."

Sam laughed aloud at this. "To Robert, even Cambridge seems too wild a place for a daughter of his, I think. Yet we have our own college, which must be as fine as any in the world!"

I was glad that my cousin was left behind. Annie was just a year older than I was, even if she stood a full head taller at the time. And I loved the stories she told.

"Tell us about your sail from England," I begged of her as we rode that morning.

"Most everyone on the ship grew sick, even the captain and his crew," she began. Her voice was as loud as if she were trying to win the attention of the thick horse that pulled our wagon. "Two children and a man died before reaching Boston. It was most horrible. Their faces were blue and blown up like a pig's bladder. I saw them myself." To demonstrate, she pinched her nose and filled her cheeks. I laughed to see her bloated face. "You wouldn't laugh if you had seen them. And when the captain had their bodies put overboard, they did not sink into the ocean but floated there, bobbing in the waves. The captain said that this proved their souls were wicked, but my father said that this was foolish talk. Men cannot know why God chooses to take some men into heaven sooner than others. Or why a body floats or sinks. That's what my father said."

James grew solemn. What Annie had said touched something in him. "There is so much that men cannot know," he said. "My mother died when I was younger than Bartholomew. No kinder woman lived in all the world than she, but I do not know, even to this day, why she was taken while others who were wicked stayed behind."

"What did she die of?" I asked.

"The English pox," he said. "I suffered from it, too. I was very small, yet I remember lying too weak to move upon a bed of skins in our great house of birch bark and bent willow branches. But my mother was sicker than I. Touching her, I felt my fingers might burn, and later she turned cold. She died, along with half the people of our village. When she died and I did not, my father said that this was a sign of my good fortune, that something was expected of me. But I did not find any happiness in it. And soon after, I was taken away."

Never before had I heard him speak of his mother. I never even stopped to think that he must have a mother. Now, I had a host of questions for him, but Annie did not give me a chance to speak.

"Is your mother now in heaven?" she asked. This was a constant concern of all of us—who would go to heaven and who would not.

"I pray she is," he said. "But she was not baptized. No Indian could be in those days."

I was struck by his sudden sadness. It was as if his mother had died just yesterday and not twenty years before. And I began to think how terrible it would be never to see my own mother again, not in this life or even in the next.

Soon, however, our somber mood was broken as we reached the bridge that crossed the Charles. The sun was risen in the sky, just a few short steps above the earth. The river did not smell of terrible things, as it does now, and a breeze swept upon us, full of the scent of sweet blossoms as we rode high across the swollen waters. There were boats upon the river and waterfowl of all varieties, ducks and coots and tumbler birds.

Slowly we left the muddy riverbank behind us and turned toward Boston. How peaceful it was this day. And it was beginning to be warm in the dappled sunlight. We moved toward a farmhouse set off like a castle behind a low, uneven wall of rocks and boulders cleared from the fields. There were no signs of the farmer or his cattle. Ahead, off to the other side, we could see an orchard of apple and nut trees, still full of flowers and alive with all manner of insects.

And then I heard a rush of air and felt a sudden sting on my forehead. And then another whoosh and a sting upon my arm. These were not bees, but rocks and stones arching through the air, falling down upon us like hail from the heavens. Annie surprised me by turning toward me and covering me with her body, but not before I felt another hit and another and another. I felt a little river of blood flowing down my face, as if a dam were broken.

"Ooo," said my cousin when a rock struck

the back of her head. And the fusillade of rock, pebble, and stone kept falling.

James leaped from the wagon and rushed toward the wall, straight into the barrage. Suddenly the stones stopped, and a dozen figures stood and ran from him. It was as if he were a hunter and had flushed a covey of quail, so suddenly did they appear and race away.

I saw them scatter across an open field and head for the woods beyond. They were boys, all of them, some smaller than myself, dressed in tattered clothing of sad colors. James jumped over the wall and was catching up with the slowest of them, a small, capless boy. The child was just within James's reach when a door was flung open from the farmhouse, and an old man walked out. His white hair was only partly covered by his tall hat. The musket he carried so unsteadily in his hands was as long as he was.

"Leave the boy alone, heathen!" he shouted. His voice was pitched high as a flute. The gun he lifted to his eye so that he might aim it.

James stopped still in the middle of the field, but his quarry did not. The boy kept running for the woods where he soon vanished with the others.

James stood frozen, like a rabbit cornered by a dog. He dared not twitch as the farmer walked toward him.

Annie said to me, "Stay where you are! I must help him!" and she jumped down from the high wagon seat and ran for James. I followed close behind her, ignoring my injuries. I could feel the cool blood upon my forehead.

She was far faster than I was and quick over the wall and into the field. "Do him no harm!" she yelled again and again. "You must do him no harm!"

I could not believe what I saw because she ran straight for the man and, to his surprise, boldly grabbed on to his musket and pulled it from his hands the way a mother might take a pointed stick from her baby.

"I won't let you harm him!" she said.

The man was more startled than angry to be treated so by a young girl. "No Indian may lay his hand upon an English child while Goodman Harry Frost is able to stop him," he said. But his voice was now a broken note.

"He had good cause," my cousin said. And

she pointed to me as evidence. I stood breathless before them, the blood smeared and clotted about my face. "Look what these terrible children have done!" Annie said.

"And who are you," the man said, "to be riding with an Indian on a Saturday morn in times like these?"

"I am Annie Clark, and this man is James Printer, apprentice to my uncle, Samuel Green."

"Looks like no apprentice I have ever seen," Goodman Frost replied. "He's but an Indian sneaking about, dressed up in English clothes."

"You are partly right in that," James said, smiling now. "I *am* an Indian dressed in English clothes, but also an apprentice."

"And talks like an Englishman, too!" said Goodman Frost. This seemed to surprise him more than the clothing.

"I was reared in the house of Master Henry Dunster and his good wife, at Harvard College," James said. "And it was there that I began to learn the craft of printing. They kept the college presses in their house in those days and treated me as one of their own."

Goodman Frost was befuddled. "Well, well," he said. "I remember Master Dunster. Some thought him a fool, but he never harmed me."

Annie became impatient and turned the barrel of the gun toward its master. "You might have killed poor James!" she shouted. Old Harry Frost stood trembling.

"Now, now, Annie," said James. "Goodman Frost meant no harm to me."

"That's true," the man now said in his own defense. "I saw an Indian clothed like an Englishman, chasing a boy across my field, and what was I to think? My first thought was that he was an evil savage and wanted to scalp that little fellow."

"That boy and the others might have killed us with their stones!" Annie said, still holding the long gun. "Look at him," she said, pointing at me. "He is the one who is wounded."

"But you cannot blame the boys," Goodman Frost said. "There are so many stories about savages who steal and rob from us English and would gladly kill us in our sleep for a few shillings or a bottle of West Indies rum."

James took the musket gently from Annie's hands and returned it to the old man, who seemed surprised to have it back.

"In future, Goodman Frost, you will use this to guard the safety of innocent travelers along this road and not a mob of ruffian boys who attack them," he said.

James turned and walked away, with the two of us following behind him. We left the old man muttering to a flock of crows that had settled in the field.

Once back at our wagon, I said, "You have saved James, Annie. How brave you are!"

"There was nothing brave," she said. "I did not stop to think. Besides, old Harry Frost did tremble so, he could not have fired his musket straight."

"Goodman Frost did not mean to injure me," James said. But it was Annie he first helped up onto the wagon, though I was the injured one.

When all three of us were again seated upon our high perch, Annie carefully cleaned my face with a white handkerchief that turned red in her hands. My head was tender to the touch, but the sight of my own blood upon the white cloth hurt more than my wounds.

"Why did those boys throw stones at me?" I asked her.

"Why, Bartholomew, they were not throwing at you!" she said. "It's James they wanted to harm."

CHAPTER TWO

THE INDIAN KING

IN SILENCE AT FIRST, WE ROLLED TOWARD Boston. I could not keep my gaze from James. I saw him now with fresh eyes.

"How did you come to be English, James?" I asked.

Annie laughed at my question, but James did not. Instead, he lifted his head a little, as if he were looking for an answer in the distance before he finally replied.

"I was a boy younger than you, when my

mother died," he said. "It was then that the Reverend John Eliot rode into our camp upon a large gray horse that seemed to be breathing smoke and fire. Before that day, I was only a person in my mind, not English or Indian. My family is Nipmuck. It means people of the rivers, for my people lived upon the flowing water. They traveled in bark canoes so light that one man could carry upon his back a boat large enough for six.

"Today Master Eliot is an old man, bent and gray, but then he was straight and lean like a tall and slender alder. I can see him before me, with his neat-cut hair without a single strand of silver. His nose looked like a protruding beak, and he often made a joke of it. He'd say it was right that he looked like a hawk, because he was a bird of prey. And pray he did, so often that every other sentence was a prayer.

"But what I noticed first were his eyes. They were a clear blue like the waters of a deep pond. And when he looked down upon me from his horse, I felt his eyes did cut and peer inside. I knew from the first that he wanted to take something from me and put something else in its place.

"My father gathered everyone before Master Eliot and at a signal from him, my father and the rest fell to their knees. And then the preacher passed out gifts to everyone. There were clay pipes and tobacco for the adults, who began to smoke all at once. And for the children there were apples and honeycomb and little bits of ribbon and cloth, or beads strung together on a cut of leather.

"But I cared not for any of these things. I looked instead at a strange object that Master Eliot held in his hands. It was a thing covered in leather and divided into thin, white pieces like leaves. This was the Englishman's magic. A book, my father said it was. There was no word for it in Algonquian but 'book,' same as in English.

"Master Eliot stopped his speaking and showed me a leaf with its scratches, black upon white. And he said that these were words that told stories older than the father of his father and if I listened, I could hear them.

"To me this was magic, and I told him that I wanted nothing more in the world than to know how to hear those words for myself. And he promised that he would teach me.

"Now, my brothers were there, too, and they laughed at the way Master Eliot spoke our tongue. And my father said that they must show respect to this Englishman. But my brother Anaweakin rose to his feet and took out his knife and rushed at Master Eliot.

"With one hand, he held Master Eliot by the throat, with the other he pressed a long knife against the preacher's chest. And Anaweakin asked if Master Eliot's lord was powerful enough to keep him from cutting out his heart. But my father told my brother to put his knife away, because the English had many more muskets than we did and they surely would destroy us if any harm came to so great a man as Master Eliot.

"My brother did as he was told, saying 'It is *I*, not your lord, who has let you live,' but we were all impressed by Master Eliot's courage. And I thought how powerful was the English God to stop my brother from killing him.

"Later that day, my father told me that my orphaned cousin, Wampus, and I were to go with the preacher to live with the English.

And on the spot Master Eliot gave us both our Christian names. Wampus became John, and I, Wowaus, became James.

"Master Eliot took us by horseback to the home of Henry Dunster, who was the president of Harvard College in Cambridge. I remember seeing his house, one story stacked upon the other, with pointed roofs and windows of glass. And I thought surely the English king himself lives here.

"Mistress Dunster took us in. She was a small woman, pale and a little wrinkled, but with very strong hands that kept their grip on us. I had never seen the inside of such a house before. And I saw how the English set their fires upon stone hearths, and how they sat on chairs raised up above the ground. Most marvelous of all was a small mirror that hung upon a wall in the kitchen. In it I could see a dark face, streaked with dirt, the hair greased with bear fat and tied with bits of ribbon and cloth. John and I laughed at these sad, dirty boys. No one would think that they could be English.

"She made us stand still in the kitchen, while she walked around us, all the time wrinkling her nose at the look and smell of us. Next she had her servants strip away our deerskin clothing and lift us up into a large metal pot near the fireplace. They began to pour kettles of steaming water about us. And I wondered if we were being cooked up into a stew. But instead we were soaped and scrubbed with brushes, then dried off and dressed in cloth of black and gray and white. Finally she chopped off our hair and brushed it out.

"Then she held a mirror up to us and let us see that we were made over completely. With only a little more soap and hot water, I thought that even our skins would grow pale and we would be the same as any English boys.

"It is an odd thing, but when I saw myself scrubbed clean in English clothes, I knew for the first time that I was different from the English, that I was an Indian."

I could not wait for him to tell the rest of his story but had to ask him, "How did you learn to speak English just the way we do?"

"My cousin John and I were taken to the charity school, but I think I learned English sitting at Mistress Dunster's table," James said. "Her sons ate with us, and there were always two or three college students who came to join us. I listened closely, especially to the arguments among them. And it was not long before I spoke just the way the Dunsters did."

We were getting close to Boston now. Sitting high upon my father's cart, we began to see more people. But instead of greeting them with good cheer, I saw them with suspicion. Who among them wanted to harm James, I wondered, just because he was an Indian?

Finally, we left the rutted road and turned into city lanes paved in stone.

And I noticed how the clothing had changed. Here many men wore capes and caps of bright color, and puffed upon clay pipes as they walked through the streets. And the women were dressed as brightly, in dresses decorated with delicate lace and colored ribbon.

"How lovely they are," Annie said, "like so many flowers, no two of them alike. I told you it would be so, didn't I, Bartholomew?"

But my eyes were open now, and I noticed things that Annie did not. There were boys and girls in tattered clothing; and haggard men, several missing arms and one a leg; and many soldiers carrying long guns. Here, too, were frightful bearded men in deerskin costume, trappers come to exchange their goods. And there were foreigners speaking strange, burbling tongues.

James pulled up our cart before the shop of Master Hezekiah Usher, the bookseller, who greeted us as heartily as if we had come all the way from England itself.

"I hope your journey was a pleasant and comfortable one," he said. He spoke to me before saying a word to James, as if I were a man of great importance like my father.

"Yes, sir," I said, "except that we were attacked by ruffians along the way."

"It was James who was attacked," said my cousin, "because he is plainly Indian."

"But it was I who was injured!" I proclaimed.

Master Usher took careful notice of me, touching my forehead and examining my wound. For all the blood, the damage was small, a little nick no wider across than a farthing. Still, he shook his head and sucked several times on his lips, making a kissing sound that meant his disapproval. "Ruffians, they were," he said. "Many such ruffians have we here in Boston these days."

He turned to James to ask, "I trust no harm has come to you, Goodman Printer?"

"None at all, thank you, Master Usher," James said.

"Oh, but that old farmer might have shot you!" said Annie.

Again, Master Usher made that kissing sound in the air. "Great burning wars are made from such little sparks as these," he said. "Calamitous days in calamitous times. But we have work to do."

He pulled a single book from the cart and unwrapped it from its paper. He turned it over and over in his hands, looking at the leather cover and the careful stitching of the binding. "I see your handiwork in this, Goodman Printer. It is sewn together as tightly as a lady's skirt."

And then he gently opened the book, oohing and aahing as his fingers marked the straight lines of type. "This is good, this is good," he said. "A book that sings as sweetly as the songs within."

Soon we emptied the load of books into a small storeroom. The shelves were already nearly filled with many books that were printed in Cambridge in my father's shop and others shipped in from London at considerable expense. I recognized an almanac, and a story of a shipwreck, and a history of New England, and a volume about the London fire and plague—all printed by S. Green, my father, who set his own name into type upon each title page. There were sermons and hymnbooks, too.

We carefully stacked the newest volumes in the space that Master Usher had saved for them. When we were done, he gave me a pail and a handful of pennies and directed me to a nearby tavern. "A good morning's work leaves a body dry," he said. "Tell the mistress at the Three Boars to fill this with her best beer."

The way to the Three Boars was crooked, and I thought I might be lost more than once. People were everywhere, but all too busy with purposes of their own to help a boy find his way in their hectic city. But soon I found the sign of three beasts with hairy backs and sharp tusks that were meant to be wild boars.

Inside, I handed my pail to a large woman with stout, bare arms who wore upon her face a habitual smile. The air within was rich with smells, of cakes and breads and beers, of all things made with yeast. As I waited for the pail to be filled, I looked about and saw idle men sitting around long tables. Some had children with them. And I saw that a small boy pointed at me and that all the men at that table took notice. One was a man with a torn coat, who stared at me with a single eye, for there was a patch upon the other. The man's good eye ran up and down me, like a tailor sizing me for a new suit of clothes. A ragged scar divided his face, which drooped in a perpetual scowl, broken teeth showing between his gaping lips. "A boy that loves Indians, are you?" he shouted.

I was so afraid that I could not speak. The boy must have been one of the ruffians who threw stones upon us.

"Answer when you're spoken to, boy," the man said.

"Oh, leave the child alone, Lemuel Brown," the mistress of the tavern said as she handed me back the pail, brimming now with frothy beer.

"It was an Indian who gave me this," the man replied, pointing to the patch. "And so it is that I have no use for Indians or for those who travel with them." He rose to his feet. He was a tall man, even without his hat, and he walked toward me with a grimy hand outstretched.

"Go, boy," the woman said, grabbing my shoulders and steering me toward the door. But Lemuel Brown stood before me, his face in mine, and reached for the patch as if to lift it.

But before he could, the tavern mistress bowled him out of the way. Sprawled upon the floor, he seemed more comical than menacing, and I laughed at him.

"Laugh if you must at this torn remainder of a man, but I'll remember you and your Indian friend," he said.

I ran down the narrow streets back to Master Usher's shop, splashing beer upon my path. The pail was half foam by the time I set it down again.

Annie stood alone in the shop.

"Master Usher has asked me to mind things until he and James finish their work in back," she said cheerily. "And you can help." There was nothing Annie wanted as much as to be left in charge of things.

But we had little to do until a tall man walked in, carrying a long gun, which he put down by the door.

Annie curtsied.

The man before her was a person of dark mood and frozen expression, one of those people who might keep his head down as he walked in hope that no one could speak to him and demand that he be cheerful.

"I am come for a book," he said, not bothering with the usual greetings or politeness.

"Then you, sir, have come to the right place," Annie said, teasing him. She smiled so hugely that it might have brightened a dark room, but he took no notice of her.

"It's a book of hymns that I want," the man said.

"Oh, sir, we have just the book for you, newly printed in Cambridge," she said.

Just then, James walked in with an armload of those very books. Annie plucked one of them away and tried to hand it to the stranger.

The man did not reach for the book but looked instead at James. And his expression, so glum before, changed to agitation and alarm.

"You are not an Englishman," he declared.

"In that, you are correct, sir," James said, placing the remaining books on a convenient shelf.

"And you have touched these books, sir!" the man said.

"Yes, that is true," James said. He did not appear puzzled, but I was.

"You have touched a sacred book!" the man said, his anger growing. "It is a defilement!"

"A defilement it is not, as you should well know, Captain Samuel Moseley, sir," said Master Usher, entering now with an armload of books.

"Still," said the captain, "I will take one of these instead." And the soldier plucked a book from the bookseller's arms.

The captain seemed pleased as he turned the little volume in his hands. How fine such a book feels to the touch with its soft deerskin cover. "How much will that be, Master Usher?" he said.

"Eight shillings for you," the store owner said.

"That seems rather dear," said Captain Moseley, now opening the book and seeing the handiwork of my father's shop. He reached into his jacket, pulled out his purse, and stacked the full amount upon a counter. With the book clutched in one hand, he grabbed his musket with the other and left us.

Annie began laughing, and when she laughed, with her voice as rich and high as any singer's, everyone could not help but laugh with her. And so we all did, James and Master Usher with the two of us children, not giggling or tittering, but with much heaving and bending over. "Oh, James," she said. "He did not want you to touch the book. But did you not touch every page of it in the printing?"

"There is not a page that I did not feed into the press," he said.

"The captain does not know, and I will not tell," said Master Usher, who now helped himself to the beer, or what was left of it after my hurried run through the streets. He was flushed and giddy. "Oh, Captain Moseley is a fiercesome soldier, most brave and honorable," he said. "But I think he has but little wit. And for that reason did I charge him eight shillings for that pretty new book of songs instead of six, which is the price for other, gentler persons."

Our business in Boston was not finished when we left the bookseller. Our printing shop devoured paper, which had to be shipped from London, and we were to fetch one hundred reams newly arrived in the port. Flags of many nations flew from the ships anchored in the harbor and snapped in the wind. Along the wharves, brawny men lifted huge casks and crates with block and tackle and lowered them into wagons.

The paper came in large sheets, packed into crates for shipment. And our poor horse, who I thought the strongest in the world, strained against the load. The wharves of Boston were little compared to what they are today, but to me they seemed splendid enough. I had to lean back in my seat to see the mast tops of the ships, these no different from the ones that brought my father to this same place full forty years before.

As we slowly rolled through the streets of the port, I spotted an odd figure of a man, an Indian dressed in foolish finery of women's ribbons and bits of lace, of gold buttons and turkey feathers stitched upon a bright blue English coat. He carried a large, round sack over one shoulder. I pointed to him, and after one look, Annie and I could not help but laugh to see this dark-skinned, prancing dandy of a man. James preferred not to look at all, but to mind the horse and reins.

Annie and I were not the only ones to laugh. A mob of English children, idle boys, mostly, tagged after him. "Your Royal Highness!" they shouted, doffing their hats to him. "Your majesty!"

"And who is this majesty?" I asked. "James, do you know him?"

"No kin of any king I know," said Annie, laughing at the antics of this mock monarch, who carried himself proudly, smiling at the rabble that taunted him as if they were gathered to amuse him.

"Oh, he is a king and a king's son," James said, "as truly a monarch as our own King Charles, though of a smaller realm."

"Look at the wampum about his neck," Annie shouted, pointing to the Indian's enormous necklace of white and blue shells. These were the pounds and shillings of Indian currency, and could be exchanged for English money. Like some rich English merchant wearing necklaces of gold, he was wearing his fortune for all to see.

"Who is he, James?" I begged. "Please tell us who he is."

But before he could answer, the "Indian

majesty" took notice of us, sitting high upon our cart. Ignoring the mob that surrounded him, the man fixed his eyes upon James and walked directly toward him. The ruffian children followed after him.

He stood in the path of our wagon. The horse reared up and then stopped. The Indian walked to the side of the wagon, put his sack on the ground, and reached for James's arm as if he intended to pull him off the cart. He succeeded only in bringing their two faces close together.

"What is your name?" the Indian dandy asked in ordinary English.

"James."

"I know of you," he said. "You are James the printer. You are a Nipmuck. I know your father and your brothers well."

James said, "I am the one you speak of."

The Indian had the most terrible expression upon his face, a fiercesome look where moments before there had been a tight and idiotic grin.

"You know who I am?" the Indian asked.

"I know you," James said. "The English call you King Philip."

I should have known him all along. My father often complained of this Philip, the Indian sachem who wore women's ribbons and lace and claimed to be the equal of our own King Charles. He was given the English name in jest when but a boy, after a royal Greek, Philip, the king of Macedonia and father of the great Alexander. My father said that he ran up debts among the English merchants and then refused to pay them.

The Indian did not let go of James, who held tight to the cart to keep from tumbling down. The little mob of children kept shouting out advice. "He's a king, all right," one boy said. "King of the savages."

"It does not trouble me if the English laugh at me," King Philip said, tightening his hold on James as he spoke. "They look upon me and see what it is they wish, a wild heathen, a child in love with bits of lace and bright cloth. Let them think me a crazy fool; I want them to. But you will speak of me as Metacom, sachem of the Pokanokets. My father was Massasoit, who knew this land before the English. My brother was killed by them. The day will come when no one of us is safe in our own land. And whatever clothes we wear, we cannot hide, for they will know us by our skin." He placed a hand on top of James's hand, both the same shade of brown. "One day I will call for you, and you will come."

And then, as suddenly as he had grabbed him, Philip let James go. He stood for a minute looking at us. It was then I noticed the large tomahawk with rounded stone and the long knife he carried on his belt—one to bash the skull of an enemy, and the other to take his scalp.

He bent to pick up his sack. I could not help myself. I had to know what was in it. "What do you carry?" I asked him.

Philip smiled at me and at the band of ruffian children as he reached into his bag and pulled out what looked like a ball covered in fur. Then he reached in again and brought out a second. With his arms outstretched above his head, he turned so that everyone could see. In each hand, he held the severed head of a wolf. Whatever beauty there might have been in these animals was gone now. The hair was dirty and matted. They stared at us through dull and sunken eyes.

"Once each year, I must take five of these to Plymouth, to fulfill the pledge I made when I agreed to keep the peace with the English," he said to James.

"And what do the English do with them?" James asked.

"They mount them upon poles and make great ceremony and mock my people, the Pokanokets."

"So why do you continue?"

"Better a wolf's head upon a pole than mine." The sachem laughed heartily at his own joke. "Better a wolf's head than an old Indian's."

Quickly, he returned the heads to the bag, picked it up, and marched away, the mob of children following after him.

"He frightens me," said Annie.

I was frightened, too, but did my best not to show it. "Father says that he's a weakling and a fool," I said as confidently as I could.

James looked at me severely. "Philip is not a weakling or a fool," he said. "And we would be wise to treat him like the king he is and not make him angry."

He clucked to the horse, which strained against the load and took us home.

CHAPTER THREE

SOUNDS OF WAR

IT WAS THE JOB OF MY HALF-BROTHER, SAM, to make me a printer. Sam was a large man, grown powerfully strong from working the presses every day, with bulging arms and a chest like the trunk of a giant sycamore. There was no more kindly man in the world when the work of the day was done and he had time to talk and joke about. But he also had another side, as if two separate people lived inside the one body. This other Sam was quick to anger and had no patience for a mere printer's devil.

One late spring evening, some weeks after I first saw King Philip, Sam sent the letters flying at my head like bullets. If they could have spoken, they would have sounded out whole sentences of harsh warning and stern advice.

In the year since I began to work as a printer's devil, I had made a poor beginning.

"You have forgotten all I taught you," he said.

He was wrong about that. He had taught me to hide from him when he was angry, a lesson I never forgot. Now I dodged the tiny pieces of lead and did my best to hide behind a table full of printed pages neatly stacked.

"Shiftless boy!" he yelled. "Half a brother of mine, but all the wit and brains from that other half!"

Now that was more than I could bear. This insult was aimed not just at me but at my mother, Sarah Clark Green, who was my father's second wife. She was two years younger than Sam, but mistress of my father's house. He was bound to be obedient to her and even to call her Mother. Yet this did not sit well with Sam, who seemed to be always picking quarrels with her.

There was no gentler person in all the world than my mother. She could not lift a rod against me, her firstborn son. If that was a fault, then it suited me just fine.

Now Sam had insulted her and I could not let it pass. "Half-brother! Half-wit!" I said. "Whole villain! Full knave! And fool complete!"

No boy of that time could say such a thing to an elder and not expect to be punished.

Sam reached for a willow switch. There was a good supply of them in the print shop, for just such an occasion as this.

What a sight we must have been, in the glow of burning candles, among the presses and tables in the printing room of the old Indian school at Harvard College. Here a stout man advanced toward a slight boy who stood as still as he could, flinching before the punishment that was due him.

Just then the far door opened and James walked in.

He wore no hat over hair as straight and gleaming black as if he had combed it with bear grease. I was glad to see him.

"What's this I hear, Bartholomew?" he asked in the pleasant voice of an English gentleman. "I could hear your voice all the way to your father's house. If your gentle mother were in her bed, your quarrel has surely wakened her."

The shop was next to Harvard College, in a two-story building called the Indian college, although Indians studied there no longer. Now the brick edifice was home to a few English students, who slept upstairs, and to my brother, Sam, who had a small room above our shop. As an apprentice, James slept in the shop itself, between the press and the hearth, the better to start work early and stay on late.

My father and mother's house, as James did know, was in the town, a full half-mile away near the creek road. My voice could not have carried so far, even on a calm, spring night.

But James's words shamed me.

As for Sam, he laughed as if the whip of willow in his hand were nothing more than a jest and put the branch away.

"It was but a friendly debate between loving brothers," he said.

"Enemies do not always cut so deep," James said. "What was the cause of your quarrel?"

"He has confused his 'p's' and 'q's' again," Sam said, sure that James would know just how terrible such mistakes could be in a printing shop. "And his 'b's' and 'd's,' and has them so often turned about that two cases of letters need re-sorting. I wonder that he will ever become a printer."

This hurt me as much as any piece of type thrown by my brother. There was nothing on earth I wanted more than to be a printer, like my half-brother and my father. Like James. My mother wanted me to sit all day in school, to become a minister as my Uncle Robert had. But I could not sit still for school and I fidgeted in churches. My dream was to rise in the printer's craft from devil to apprentice to journeyman and to master. I wanted to see my own name upon a title page, "printed by Bartholomew Green." But the lead letters used in the press were all reversed, as if they had been copied from a looking glass, and even after a year I did not know how anyone could read them.

"He will learn to sort type soon enough, if guided by a strong but kindly hand," James said.

"I have no patience for him, I'm afraid," Sam said. "James, won't you take over his instruction? For you can calmly see his faults when I cannot. Let us see what *you* can make of this bent piece of a boy."

"There is no better time to begin than now," James replied. "Before the candles are snuffed out for the night, he will make both these cases right."

"And pick each piece of type off the floor," Sam added. "For he is the cause of the rage that sent it there."

I was about to object, but James spoke first. "Of course, he will find every last piece. And once done, I will teach him the trick of reading type, how each letter is different from the other and how to know them all by touch as easily as sight."

Just then the door opened again, letting in a gust of springtime air along with my cousin Annie and an old woman.

"Good gentlemen!" the woman said. "I have a tasty cider for you tonight." It was Goodwife Gray, who each night at the same hour brought a bucket of ale or cider to the shop. Her nose and cheeks were covered in spidery red marks, the little signs, it was said, that she sipped too much of the drinks she brewed.

Sam took a full cup of cider, drank it down in a gulp, and then took another. He sat sprawled upon a chair near the fireplace, his day's work done. When Goody Gray offered a cup to James, he refused it as he always did. He drank only water, and took that plain, without sugar or spice, the way I learned to like it, too.

Now Goody sat down opposite Sam by the fireplace, with a large cup of her own brew in her hands, so the two of them could exchange gossip from around our town. Nothing happened that Goody did not know, it seemed.

James bustled around the shop, making it clean and ready for another day, as I crawled about looking for each missing letter. Then James stooped down with me, to begin going through the little compartments of type, as Annie watched over us.

"The little barbs and flourishes, the serifs, set

each letter apart," James explained. "Once you know them, there is no mistaking a 'b' for a 'd.' You can read them with your fingertips."

I began to study the two letters, taking my time and not rushing the way I always had before. "I see it," I said at last. "I can tell them apart."

James took one of each letter and put his hands behind his back. Then he held out a large, brown fist and opened it. This was a workman's hand, large-knuckled and callused. The little bit of lead seemed even smaller in his palm than mine.

"Which is it?" he asked. And I knew the piece of type was a "b"; there was no mistaking it. Soon he had scrambled all the difficult letters, and I found it easy to tell them apart.

"Now you will have no trouble setting all the type case right," he said.

I began doing so, pleased with myself for learning so quickly. But my cousin Annie, who had been watching the whole time of my lesson, had a different view.

"You are so slow," she said. She took the tray of type from my hands and quickly began to sort through it, picking out letters that were out of place.

She had learned by watching, and already was quicker than I.

James was delighted. "Soon enough the two of you will be as good as master printers, and I will be able to sit idle while you do the work of the day."

As the two of us sorted the type, James joined Goody and Sam by the fire.

"What news do you bring us, Goody?" James asked.

She sat in a wobbly chair, rocking back and forth, ready to ladle up the news she had gathered as she made her evening rounds through the college and the town. Before there were newspapers in New England, we relied on Goody for our news.

"Much news, this night," said Goody Gray. "Have you heard of the three Indians held at Plymouth for murdering John Sassamon, the Indian teacher?"

"I knew John Sassamon," Sam said. "He was a well-spoken man, and I was sorry to hear that he was killed last winter."

"I never did like him," Goody confessed. "He was such a sour-faced man, and liked to pretend to be better than he was born. He was always sneaking around the college as if he belonged here. And him a savage in English clothes."

I looked at James when she said this. Did she think our James was but a savage in English clothes? I could not tell if James paid her any attention, for at this moment he rose for a drink of water.

"They say these Indians killed this Sassamon because he was too friendly with the English. They say King Philip was behind it," Goody said, shaking her head as she spoke. "For you know that King Philip called him an English spy and wanted him killed."

"But what of the three murderers?" Sam asked. "They were the ones you were going to tell us about."

"Two of them are dead," said Goody, pleased that no one present had heard this news. "As for the third, when he was hanged, the rope broke neatly in two, and so he lived to be hanged another day."

"Then there will be a war," Sam said.

For weeks in my mother's house, there had been hushed talk of war, and King Philip was at the center of it. I dreamed of him, covered in ribbons and lace, the wampum belt about his neck, and holding the wolves' heads high above his own. I shivered at the thought of him.

"There will be a war," Goody agreed. "There are signs of it everywhere. Have you seen the comet in the sky? Now, I myself have not. My poor eyes fail me, but people with far better eyes tell me it's there, so it must be so. And in Boston, it is said, a baby was born with lizard skin and horns upon its back. I have not seen this child, you understand, but I heard it direct from someone who heard it from her cousin, who saw it herself. And you've heard what happened near Mendon. There was a chicken hatched that had two heads. These are omens of great events. War and rebellion are sure to be coming soon." She rocked back in her chair, pleased with herself for bringing us word of coming calamity.

"If there be a war, it will be a short one," Sam said. "The Indians are no match for the English. We will drive them from New England if they dare to take arms against us."

Annie spoke up. "My father says that the Indians have many just complaints against the English, who take their property and give them trinkets and ale in exchange. He says that those who have lost everything can be the most terrible foes."

"Not against our English muskets," Sam said.

James picked up a rag and wiped the printing press clean again, leaving it polished and gleaming. He took pride in his craft, in the printing of words upon paper. Surely, no one would want to drive him from New England, I thought.

"If there is a war, King Philip will not start it," James said. "He believes that whoever draws first blood must lose, and he will not strike first."

"Oh, he's a fool," said Goody.

"Do not be mistaken about him," James said. "He is no fool. He is wiser than he seems."

Goody Gray reddened, the color spreading across her cheeks as if ignited by her red nose. Custom did not allow an Indian man, no matter how well he had been taught in English ways, to speak like that to an English woman, even one who earned her living by the penny selling ale by the pint.

"Be careful how you speak," she warned him, "to old Goody Gray." To this, James again grew silent as he wiped the presses one more time.

After finishing a third cup of Goody's cider, my brother, Sam, was excited. "If there is to be fighting, then I will be the first to go," he said.

I could see him marching into battle with a musket upon his shoulder. And I said, "Oh, I wish I could go with you."

"Will many scalps be taken?" Annie asked. She and I had seen an old man who had lost his scalp in the war against the Pequots. He wore a funny patch of fur on top of his head. Sometimes, to entertain small children, he took it off to show an oblong spot that was covered with neither hair nor skin, but just plain bone.

"A good many scalps will be lost," answered Sam. "English and Indian alike, I am afraid."

Goody Gray touched her cap. "No one would want these old gray locks," she said. And then she laughed. I trembled to think that my own sandy hair could be hanging on an Indian belt or trophy stick.

"If there is a war," I said, "I shall ask Father for a musket of my own."

"And I will have one, too," said Annie.

Goody Gray drained another cup of her own cider and was feeling very jolly. "No Indian will be safe if you two are called to arms," she said, rocking with laughter.

Now the door opened, and my father, Master Samuel Green the senior, entered. Every night he came by to inspect the printing shop and see that all was in order.

"You burn my candles by the dozen," he said, and began snuffing half of them out one after another, pinching the flames with his fingers.

The evening air was cool, and my mother had seen that he wore a red cloth cap, and a scarf about his throat. He threw off the scarf and tossed the cap upon a writing table. His head shone as if it had been oiled and polished.

He was a hardy man of sixty, even stouter than my brother, Sam. He took a chair by his accounting desk and pulled out a ledger.

I ran up to him. "There's to be a war with the Indians, Father," I said. "Sam says so."

"Believe it not," he said. "For we taught

them a lesson in the Pequot war. No Indians want to risk the wrath of good, God-fearing Englishmen."

"But the two Indians were hanged," I said.

"Harsh justice will prevent a war," he said, "and not encourage it. And Master Eliot's Bible will not wait for a war. You know what that means to us? A new translation of Master Eliot's Indian Bible in the Algonquian tongue?"

"Endless trouble," said Sam, who had been a printer's devil years before when the first Indian Bible was put to press. He and James had both helped in the printing.

My father ignored Sam. "It means a great commission. Paper by the gross and ink by the barrel."

I had seen one of the old books, which was printed before I was born. How beautiful the words looked upon the page, so rich in "k's" and double "o's," the sounds that filled the Indian language.

Master John Eliot had translated it, and my father had set it into type. Now there was to be a new Indian Bible, as part of Master Eliot's plan to make Christians of all the savages.

Many believed that there would be no worry of war with the Indians if he succeeded.

"The Bible is such a fine book for a printer," my father said. "At eight pages to a sheet, one sheet per week, it's work for two and a half years. And to think, when I first came to Massachusetts Bay, I had so little to my name and no shelter from the elements. . . ."

"Except for an empty barrel," said Sam, supplying the end to the sentence. Whenever our father spoke of his progress in the world, which he did often, he began with that empty barrel. When he first came to Boston, he always told us, he had not a penny for lodging, and curled up each night in a large shipping cask and wondered whether he might freeze to death in the bitter cold of winter. We all smiled, even James.

"And now, here am I," my father said.

"A man of property," I said, knowing the speech by heart. "Printer of the laws. Clerk to the county of Middlesex. Deacon of the church. And an officer of the militia." I loved the sound of my father's many titles.

Sam laughed aloud now, his face red and grinning.

My father looked at him with a stare that might wither a prune. "You cannot know the hardship we Puritans suffered when we came new to this land. Scarce a dozen proper houses. Boston was an infant town, and Cambridge no more than a bog. Often I wondered that I might die here in the wilderness, so far from my home, as did so many others. But I put my shoulders to the work and my faith in God, and see how I have profited."

Once begun in this way, there was no stopping him until, like a clock, he had run all the way down. We all grew drowsy listening to the soothing rumble of his deep voice.

As soon as his history was done, he stood up, put on his scarf and cap, and was gone into the night. Goody Gray, walking wobbly, quickly followed. Sam left for his room, upstairs in the Indian school.

James patiently checked the type in the cases that Annie and I had sorted. He could find no mistakes. "I am impressed with your perfection," he said. "I will make printers of you both."

Annie laughed at the thought that a girl might become a craftsman. "If only I were a boy," she said. "Then I could become a printer, just like you, James."

I wished that she *could* become a boy, so that we would be printers together.

"James, when did you know you would be a printer?" I asked.

"When I lived at the Dunsters' house, they kept the college printing press in a room downstairs," James told me. "It was run in those times by the two Dayes, Stephen and Matthew, father and son. Master Dunster called them Night and Daye, because the son was so much sunnier a man than his father. It was Master Matthew who let me feed a piece of paper into the press and then helped me turn the handle. And when I pulled it out, I could see that it was full of letters and all manner of words. It was magic, surely. He said to me, 'You are a printer now.' And since that day that is all I wanted to be."

He sent my cousin and me home. The night was surprisingly cool, and the sky clear and moonless. I insisted that we stop and look for the comet that Goody told us about. We lay upon the damp ground, looking up and straining our eyes to pick out a single point from a haze of millions of stars. And to our amazement, we saw instead a shower of meteors, skimming across the sky like flat rocks bouncing upon still water. As soon as one was gone, another followed and another, hundreds of them splashing and skipping above us. And then, following the path of a shooting star, I noticed the comet, a tiny globe followed by a long tail of light—an exclamation point in the middle of the constellations.

"It is the comet, just as Goody says," I whispered, pointing to the place, hardly able to catch my breath.

"Then there will be war," Annie said softly.

We lay quietly for a while, expecting the comet to come crashing down to earth, but it did not seem to move at all. If this was a sign of horrible events to come, it should have been a larger spectacle. There should have been hot sparks and glowing lava like the volcano Vesuvius. There should be the smell of brimstone in the air. The air should roar, the earth tremble. But this was all there was, a little piece of punctuation in the sky, like the one I set at the end of this sentence! It was a disappointment. Then I heard an odd sound, a creature moving across the grass of the meadow, and then the high-pitched cry of an owl while on the hunt.

"Hear that?" I said most quietly.

"It's just an owl," Annie said, but she, too, spoke no louder than a whisper.

Gently, softly, I rolled around so that I lay flat on my belly. And so did Annie move as well. We looked in the direction of the screeching. There was something odd about the sound, like nothing any bird or animal might make. And it moved across the field, not with the quick speed of a bird in flight but with the easy amble of a man walking. And then we saw it by starlight, a dark figure gliding toward the Indian college and the printing shop, where lights still burned. It was calling out into the night, like a screech owl. I could feel a prickling in my scalp.

As it moved nearer, it took the form of a man wearing a great cape about his shoulders. Annie and I watched without speaking. I could hear my own breath now, which had become a rapid, raspy wheeze—a sound lost in the breeze that ruffled through the stiff grass of the meadow. The man—or what I now thought to be a man — moved past without noticing us, although just a few feet away. Soon he was at the door of the printing shop, which opened for him. James stood there with a candle in his hand, waiting as if he had expected this visitor. And when this stranger finally reached him, James stepped inside and closed the door behind them. All manner of trappers, traders, scholars, and ministers passed through our little town, but few at such a late hour, and fewer still signaling their arrival like a bird of prey.

"Who can it be?" I asked, finally able to breathe again.

"Let us go see," said my cousin. I wanted to do no such thing, but when she stood and walked to the printing shop, I could not help but follow her.

As quietly as we could, we tripped across the field. The two-story building had true glass windows, and those in the printing shop glowed from the candlelight within.

We looked through a window. James was speaking with a man who had his back to us. Across his broad shoulders was a great brown cloak. With an easy movement, he removed it and I could see that beneath it he wore an English jacket of bright blue, decorated all about with bits of ribbon and pieces of lace. Even from the back, I recognized him from our journey to Boston by the cut of his coat and its womanly decorations. Now he carried a musket in his hand and a powder horn at his waist along with the long knife and roundheaded tomahawk.

"King Philip!" I said, every breath now whistling through my throat.

"It is, certainly," Annie said. "What does he want of James?"

The two of them seemed to be arguing, but we could not hear about what.

All of a sudden King Philip turned around and glared toward the window. This was not the face I expected, the one I had seen by Boston harbor. It was now divided down the middle by a thick line of black paint that cut in two his forehead, nose, mouth, and chin. One side was red, the other blue. The colors made the face into a fearful mask, but it was the eyes that were most fiercesome, pitch-black circles upon a field of white.

I was sure he could see us through the glass. He was speaking loudly, spitting out his words like bitter seeds as if he were cursing every English boy who had ever taunted him.

Suddenly, he swung his body around, pulled on his cape, and bolted for the door, with James following behind as if to catch and stop him. Hardly breathing at all, I grabbed hold of Annie and the two of us hid behind a stack of firewood. James and the Indian king were outside, speaking loudly, sometimes in English and sometimes in Algonquian.

"Perhaps this war can be stopped before it has begun," James said.

"It is too late," Philip said. "The governor of Plymouth is set upon it, and will not stop until all of us are dead or sold into slavery. And I will not let happen to us what happened to the Pequots! We will not go so quietly. Wherever there are English, we will fight them. And we will take what matters most to them. It is by things that these English take their measure of a man. By houses, horses, cattle, and grain, by guns and candlesticks. All these things we will strip away until they cry out with pain. Then the time will come when a peace will be made, and that is why I need you. You can read and write the words of the English."

"I cannot go with you," James said at last. "My life is here, making words on paper for men to hear."

The other Indian laughed. "The time will come when you are as hated among them as I am hated. Then you will have no other place to go but to me. You will see. Fare thee well, James Printer. Fare thee well."

He left James standing there and marched straight in our direction. If he had found us, I don't know what he would have done. The great tomahawk that hung from his belt easily could have crushed my skull. And the long knife would have made quick work of my scalp. He walked by the woodpile, moving so swiftly that we could feel the breeze of his body as he raced by. He did not notice us at all.

When he was gone, James went inside. We waited for a few moments while he put out the candles. "We cannot say what we have seen," Annie said. "No one must know that King Philip was here."

"But why not?"

"James will be in trouble, don't you see?" Annie said.

And I did see that she was right. It was no fault of his that King Philip came to see him, but it might not be seen that way. And if there was to be a war against King Philip, James might take some blame for it. So, I did not tell my mother or my father what we had seen, although I knew it would be expected of any Puritan boy.

That night, safe in my bed, I could not seem to sleep. I could hear the breathing of my younger brothers, and felt the jostle of their every flop and turn. But later, the moon risen in the night, I dared to close my eyes. And soon I dreamed of an Indian with a face of red and blue, who grabbed me by the hair and pulled out a long, sharp knife to take my scalp. But it was not the terrible painted face of King Philip that I saw in my dream. No, the face in red and blue that I saw in my dream belonged to my friend, the printer James.

CHAPTER FOUR

FIRST FLIGHT

T HE NEXT MORNING STARTED OUT ORDINARY enough. My brother Sam often said that my tongue was like a clapper on a bell, always ringing. But this day, the clapper did not ring at all, and I told neither Sam nor my father what had happened the night before. And Annie, too, was unduly quiet. The sun not yet fully up in the sky, I was already at the printing shop, where James taught me to fill a small wooden frame, called a composing stick, with type.

These blocks of letters would later be locked into a larger frame, called a chase, from which a page was printed.

James was no different than I had known him, but I looked upon him now in a new way. I saw in his face a little bit of King Philip's face, the color the same as King Philip's, the same dark hair and eyes. Yet I could say nothing about what I had seen.

I took comfort on this day in my work. There were sticks and chases to be filled or torn apart, and the letters sorted so that they could be used again. Several times I wanted to speak to James of King Philip, but I dared not, even to him.

My day proved long and I was weary. After I became a printer's devil, there was never enough time for sleep. At nightfall, I would fall into the bed I shared with my younger brothers and plunge into my dreams the way a pebble falls into a well and then sinks into dark water. Almost nothing could wake me.

But on this night I was awakened by the steady beat of a drum, *rat-a-tat-tat*. At the same time, the church bells began ringing. Every man, woman, and child in Massachusetts Bay knew what the bells and drumroll meant. It was the call to arms. Each man of the town was to bring his musket to the meetinghouse, close by the commons.

By the time I went downstairs, my father was already dressed. He was a captain in the militia. And he carried a long gun and a lantern.

"Go fetch James and your brother, Sam, double-quick," my father said to me. "Bring them to me at the meetinghouse." Then he added. "Do not forget James. Even more than Sam, he is the one I want to see this night."

As I raced down the street and across the field toward the college and the Indian school, I could see lanterns everywhere, floating through the night, joining together, flowing in one direction.

I was running, but someone overtook me when I was halfway there.

"It's me," said Annie. "I've come to help you." I needed no help, but was glad of her company.

First we went up the stairs to rouse Sam from his room, where we found him ready with his musket in hand.

"If war is to begin, let the enemy beware," he said. He charged down the stairs ahead of us, along with the young men of the college who carried no weapons but ran as fast as Sam did.

In the printing shop, James had already heard the drum and was preparing to join the others, although he had no musket.

"Father says you are to come to the meeting-house at once," I said.

"I am just leaving now," he said.

"Has the war begun?" Annie asked.

"It is my guess that it has," he said.

"Will you fight with us or with King Philip?" I asked him.

He looked at me with puzzlement. Did he suspect that I knew who had visited him just the night before? "How can you ask, Bartholomew? I am raised with the English. I work in your shop. I eat at your table. I read the same Bible. How could I take arms against you?"

I could keep back my secret no longer. "But we saw King Philip come for you, just yesterday night," I said.

"As you can see," he said, smiling now, "I chose to stay here and be with my English family." He did not seem surprised that I knew

King Philip had been to see him. He put his hand upon my bare head and then touched Annie's hair, too. "If I must fight, it will be to see that no harm can come to you."

Then he *is* English, I thought. More than he is Indian, he is English. But how, I wondered, could an Indian be English?

As he strode toward the meetinghouse, Annie and I had to run to keep up with him.

We joined a stream of men, and boys as young as twelve, with muskets, all marching to the meetinghouse. And they were joined by the women and children of Cambridge, by servants and slaves, too. All of the students at the college mingled among them, even though they alone of the young men would not be required to go into battle. If this was the beginning of war, everyone wanted to be there to see it.

Within a few minutes, a hundred men and boys with muskets were gathered before the meetinghouse, and there were many more without guns come to join them.

My father stood upon the meetinghouse steps with a lantern in his hand. On one side of him was Master Daniel Gookin, superintendent of Indians for the colony. On the other side was the same grim-faced man we had seen at Master Usher's bookshop in Boston, Captain Samuel Moseley.

My father quieted the crowd so that Captain Moseley could speak.

"There's been an attack at Swansea," the captain said. "A farmer boy rightfully killed an Indian, one of a band that slaughtered his cattle. That was what King Philip waited for. His followers have killed nine English, striking down six unarmed men as they returned home from church. Governor Leverett has promised to send our militia to join the troops from Plymouth. Our men will march to the south at first light to seek out King Philip's lair at Mount Hope and hunt him down. The war we have feared has now begun. Let us pray tonight that the war be brief and that God protect us from our enemies in this darkest hour."

With these words, the town of Cambridge entered what we called King Philip's War.

I expected the beginning of a war to be a sorrowful thing, a time of great fear and much weeping. But Captain Moseley's small speech touched off a celebration instead. The men and children of the town began building a huge bonfire upon the commons, throwing wood and even broken furniture into the pyre. Anything that could burn was used to feed the fire, which danced to the rhythm of drums and ringing bells and clanging pots and pans. Sparks rode up into the sky on clouds of smoke. And the crush of bodies moved around the fire, as wild as any forbidden dance about a maypole.

I saw my brother Sam by the fire in celebration. And Goody Gray. And even my mother who, unlike any of the others, looked forlorn as my younger brothers rushed around, more like savages than any Indian I had known. In the crush of bodies, Annie and I stayed by James, who climbed the steps to see my father.

"Master Green," James said, "I want to volunteer. I can fire a musket and be of use in putting down this rebellion."

"Of course you shall join us," my father said.

Captain Moseley stepped forward. "The governor has said that no Indians shall be armed," he said, "for we know not in which direction they might fire their muskets. And none will be allowed to come with us, because they might betray us to King Philip."

"But surely Governor Leverett was not

speaking of loyal, praying Indians like my apprentice James," my father said. "He will make a fine soldier and help bring this war to a speedy end."

"If I had *my* way," Captain Moseley said, "no Indian would ever more be allowed to carry a gun in any of the New England colonies."

"But many would starve without muskets for hunting," James said.

"I would let them starve before I would risk the life of one English man or woman," the captain said.

"You are a harsh and impractical man," said my father. "If Governor Leverett follows your advice, he will drive our friends among the Indians to the other side and double the numbers of our enemy. Tomorrow I will make my case to the governor himself, for we cannot allow such foolish policy."

Captain Moseley now seemed very angry. He said nothing, but even by lantern light I could see that his jaw tightened. My father took James aside and spoke to him outside of the captain's hearing. "Quickly get yourself to my house and out of sight. I worry now for your safety. And you children, go with him."

Annie and I followed James as he walked down the steps in the direction of the bonfire.

Just then a great black man came up to us. His name was Lazarus, a slave who lived nearby, on Marsh Lane. My father often said that it was wrong for a man to keep another as a slave, but many families in Massachusetts Bay had slaves and considered them property, to buy and sell as they wanted. Lazarus slept in a shed behind his master's house and tended fields and cattle.

"You'd better run," he said to James.

"And why should I run?"

"I heard my master and some others talk about taking their revenge upon the Indians."

"But surely he does not mean praying Indians like myself?" James said. "I've known your master since I was but a boy."

"That's why I am telling you to run," he said. "My master said it makes no difference whether an Indian pretends to pray or not. 'We must rid ourselves of all of them, or we'll be slaughtered in our beds.' That's what he said. And be sure he will spread that word, even if it is but a lie. I'm going to flee to the north to join with the French. I see no reason to fight a war for those who keep me a slave. You can come along if you like."

"Master Green will allow no harm to come to me," James said. "And he needs me in the shop to print the laws and proclamations."

"Please yourself," Lazarus said. "I have no time to waste arguing with you."

He turned and ran.

Just then, a man came up behind James and delivered a blow to his back with the butt of a musket. James fell to his knees, his breath taken away. Above him was the grim face of Captain Moseley. "I have my eye out for you," the soldier said. And now he swung his musket again, this time aiming it for James's head.

But James saw it coming and was able to grab it before it struck. He was a strong man, as anyone is who works a press for ten and twelve hours a day or longer, and he took the musket from him. Without the gun, the captain seemed to shrink before our eyes. "Be careful of that," he said, "for it is loaded and set to fire. And harm will come to you if you use it against me." James lifted the musket to his shoulder and pointed the weapon at the captain's head. He who was a bully large just a moment before now grew small and sniveling. With a yelp, he turned and ran away with notable speed. James followed his movement with the point of his gun. There was anger in his face, a hate as deep as any Moseley held for him.

How easy it would have been for him to put a lead ball in Captain Moseley's head. And then all James's life might have been different. But Annie cried out, "No, you must not!"

James did not lower the musket at first, but said, "Be you two witness at how easy it would be for me to strike down this Captain Moseley. But I did not. Tell your father and brother of what you have seen."

Saying this he threw down the musket and began running west toward the old Indian trail that followed the river Charles.

In the days that followed, Sam went off to war. He looked fine, I thought, with his long musket resting upon his shoulder and a bright blue cap upon his head. He and my mother had made a peace between them, and when he marched away, she wept for fear of his safety.

"Shed no tears, for he will return in glory," my father said. "There is nothing to fear, for the war will be quick and victory certain."

Yet we fretted over Sam and worried about James. There was no word from either for days. News of the war was slow to come to Cambridge.

Captain Moseley stopped by our printing shop one afternoon. "Any news of my Indian apprentice, sir?" my father asked him.

"The only good news would be word of his capture," said the captain, "and I have nothing joyful to report. It is said he has run off to join King Philip. And that would not surprise me."

"That would surprise *me* greatly," my father replied. "For he is a good man and a hard worker, who has only love for the English."

"A man does not run away unless he has treachery in his heart," said the captain.

"No, but a man does run if he has reason to be frightened, sir," my father said. "For you yourself know that a frightened man does run."

My father winked at me, because I had told him the story of how Captain Moseley had struck James with his musket and then run away himself.

"I will find this James of yours and bring him back myself so that he can be properly hanged upon the commons," the captain said before wheeling around and leaving the shop.

When the captain was out of hearing, my father said to me, "Better that James be gone for a time than to see his head upon a pole, looking out on the Boston Common."

That was the custom of that time, to hang criminals upon a scaffold and mount their heads on long staffs, which would be planted on the commons.

So I worried what might become of my friend James, as late spring turned into early summer. In Cambridge, the war seemed very distant at first. But then our Indian enemies went out on a cruel and daring raid, attacking the town of Mendon, which was close by. Eight English were killed there. And soon there was talk that Cambridge itself might be assaulted.

The summer grew terrible hot, and horrible vapors rose from the swamps and rivers and ponds. The thick air was ripe with mosquitoes and stinging flies. And in some places locusts came and attacked the crops. Ministers warned that these were signs that God was displeased with us and that we English might lose the war if we did not change our sinful ways.

The troops of Massachusetts Bay and Plymouth were said to have chased King Philip and his followers into swamplands. But the Indians knew their way and the English did not, and many English soldiers were lost. What was to be a quick war and a speedy return for my brother Sam and the other Cambridge men proved to be worrisome and slow.

Then late one afternoon in early August, the bells of every church and meetinghouse rang forth. Captain Moseley himself came riding in from Boston to say that there had been a great victory in the Pocasset Swamp, and that many of our troops would parade this day in Boston upon the commons.

My father wasted no time, but mounted up his favorite horse, a gentle, spotted mare. "Might I come, too?" I asked him. And he reached down a hand to me and lifted me up and seated me before him. Loping easily along, it seemed no time before we were again in Boston. Even with so many men away at war, it was a vast and teeming town. The dusty streets were full of all manner of persons as bells pealed and cannons fired in celebration.

On the commons, the governor and his council were gathered together. "Samuel Green," a voice cried out to my father. "Master Green." It was no less than Governor Leverett himself, dressed in black except for a crimson cape that hung from his shoulders. He grabbed my father by the hand and pumped his arm.

"We have a job for our distinguished printer. We have declared a day of thanksgiving for our victory in the Pocasset Swamp, and you must print the proclamation. The Almighty has rewarded his faithful people. The war will soon be over."

"Philip is dead, then?" my father asked.

"Not Philip," Governor Leverett said. "We will have him soon enough. But our men at arms have killed three of his closest followers, including a brother. And there they are."

He pointed toward a band of armored Englishmen, who were marching toward us in high spirits, as much from ale and hard cider as from the glow of victory.

In front of this company, three of the men carried long poles straight up over them, high above the crowd that teemed about them. And upon the end of each of the three poles was the head of an Indian. Each still wore black hair upon his crown, in death just as in life. I gazed at their lifeless eyes, wondering if I would know James if I were to see him thus, his head all by itself, cut away from the rest of him.

And as I stared at these three twisted faces, their mouths gaping, their skin blackened, I felt a chill start up at my feet and travel through my body. And when it reached my neck, the world turned black as a moonless sky. Next thing I knew, the governor of Massachusetts Bay himself was pinching my cheeks as I lay upon the ground. I had fainted.

But James's was not among the heads on the commons this afternoon.

Before the day was out, my father and I were back in our print shop, setting Governor Leverett's proclamation into type. Whatever joy we might have felt was dimmed by word that my brother Sam was not among the troops sent home in triumph. And just two days later, word reached us that there had been an ambush near Brookfield, far to the west.

It was there that young Captain Edward Hutchinson was killed. My family knew him well as a friend to Sam. It was a sad time for New England, for we knew then that we might lose this war.

So there was to be no thanksgiving. Instead, my father printed up another proclamation from the governor and his council. In place of feasting and thanksgiving, there were to be fasting and a day of mourning. Governor Leverett asked that churches everywhere in Massachusetts Bay begin collecting money for the many new widows and orphans, and for those that were to come.

It looked to be a long and ugly war.

One roasting August evening, when the trees did not sway to the slightest breeze, our neighbor and friend Master Daniel Gookin came to see us at my father's house. As superintendent of the Indians for Massachusetts Bay, he still made his round of friendly Indian villages, despite the dangers in this time of war.

My father wanted him to stay with us for supper, but Master Gookin had business in Boston and wanted to travel there that very night. "Then why have you come, if you cannot tarry awhile?" my father asked.

"I have been asked to deliver this to you," Master Gookin said. And with that he handed a folded letter to my father. "I think you will find some cheer in this," he said.

It had been creased tightly and was soiled, but my father shouted with joy when he saw its source. "It is from James," he said, and proceeded to read it aloud to us all.

"When last I saw you, on the night when this terrible war began, I was running for my life. And I did run the whole night through and into morning, until my lungs burned with every breath as if there were a fire blazing in my chest. I ran west along the Indian trails, far from any thickly settled place.

"Still, to be careful, I slept by day, hidden under thickets, sharing my bed with spiders and field mice. I had the clear water of the streams and ponds to drink, but no food at all to eat. I saw no one. Except one day, I crossed the path of a young Englishwoman, carrying a basket upon her shoulders. At first she saw me

from a distance in my English coat and was not alarmed. Yet as I approached, she let out a cry, 'Heaven help us, for the savages have come to kill us!' She dropped her basket and ran from me. It was then I knew that I was right to run from Cambridge. I stopped long enough to eat a few of the berries that spilled from the basket. Then I heard the first of the musket shots and I began running again, even more wildly this time.

"Now I stayed away from trails and roads and lost myself in deepest woods. I knew only the direction of the setting sun and I followed it until I dropped for need of sleep.

"On the fourth day, I was so tired that I could not continue any farther. I climbed a slow hill and thought of my mother, these many years dead. I wondered if I might soon see her.

"Below me, the woods opened up into a farmer's field. There were men and women working in it, dressed in somber blacks and grays. They must have seen me, for there was a great commotion among them. And a small group of them came toward me with long hoes in their hands, I thought, certainly to kill me.

"I dropped to my knees and prayed. The first

voice I heard did surely surprise me. 'He is not English,' the man did say in the Algonquian tongue. 'He is an Indian.'

"There were six men before me and all were Indians like myself. 'Where am I?' I asked.

"'This is Okommakamesit,' one of them said.

"It was the praying village and plantation near the English town of Marlborough, just twelve miles from where my father and brothers lived. 'I know this place,' I said.

"And one of the men replied, 'And we know you, James the printer. Happy are we to see you.'

"Here I have stayed these many weeks and here I will remain, in safety and peace, until this war is done.

"Yet you should know that my thoughts are with you and your family, Master Green. Please send me news of your household, if you have any words to spare for me, but ask only Master Daniel Gookin to deliver them, for there are few other men who can be trusted.

"With greatest affection, I remain your obedient servant,

"JAMES PRINTER"

CHAPTER FIVE

CAPTURED

I THOUGHT OFTEN OF JAMES AND WORRIED much about Sam. Yet I had no time for idleness. These were the busiest of days in my father's shop. So busy that my cousin Annie was given as much work to do as I. Just as James had become the first Indian printer in New England, my cousin, out of necessity, became the first girl to take up that trade. My father relied on the two of us to keep up with the heavy burden of business that a war leaves for those who stay behind. Without James and Sam, he had to work doubly hard to print all the proclamations and sermons, laws and almanacs, that were required of him. And no one could turn down any job, if he wanted to be sure he would be offered another.

Printing is a difficult craft, and for a while I was of little use to the main work of our shop. To set a straight line of type was no more natural than learning to read it. My lines sagged in the middle, or slanted off at the end. For a good appearance, it is often necessary to slip little slices of lead between the words and sometimes between the letters as well. Do it slipshod, and the spaces are uneven, and the sentences seem to stutter across a page. My father had spent a lifetime setting type, and seemed to give no thought to that task. I could have tied a kerchief over his eyes, as in the game of blindman's bluff, and with only his fingers to do his seeing, he still would have been able to set lines that were regular and pleasing to behold. For my part, the more I tried to make my lines right, the more they seemed to rise and fall like musical notes.

"It is a matter of knowing your craft by

heart," Father said, talking all the while his fingers were filling a stick of type. "What the heart knows, the mind does not need to remember."

I did the best that I could, and that was not very good. Yet, for Annie, the skills came easily. Quicker and surer than I, she soon was setting type almost as fast as my father. Taller and stronger than I, she could turn the handle of the press over and over as I stood by, feeding the sheets of paper into its jaws. When I grew weary of the work, she made a game of it. When my feet and arms grew sore, she spurred me on. She had that wonderful quality of being able to find happiness and purpose whatever her fortune.

We heard little from her parents. Trappers and traders, and sometimes settlers and ministers, would carry letters from us to Annie's father and mother in Deerfield. And from time to time one of these travelers would bring us a packet of letters from them in return. The war against King Philip, for all of its wild thrashings and cruel injuries, did not reach so far to the west as Deerfield. And my uncle wrote that he thought there was greater safety there than even in Cambridge itself. "In the vast emptiness of this wilderness, Indian and Englishman do not knock into one another as they might near a city, but have room enough to live at peace," he wrote. "May it be as peaceful with you as it has been for us here."

For Annie the work in the shop gave her little time to miss her parents, who were so very far away.

My father now worked harder than he had since he was a youth. Before James and my brother left, he minded the business of the shop but did little of its labor himself. Now, he stood beside Annie and me, sweating in the summer heat. He was already by this time an old man, and in that sweltering month of August, I worried for his health. His usually ruddy face was sometimes pale with exhaustion by the end of a day. But as the summer went on, the strenuous labor seemed to restore a measure of youthfulness to his body, and his bare arms bulged with strength as he took his turn at the press.

And all the time he worked, he talked cheerfully about the good fortune that was his from the time he first arrived in New England. "Blessed," he said, "I have been blessed in my trade. Even now with battles raging, I grow more wealthy by the day." My father could find blessing in anything that made a profit, even in this horrible time of King Philip's War.

Yet we did not escape the terrors and ugliness of wartime, even in our quiet village upon the Charles. Almost every day, men would return to us from their battles. They came home most often in groups of two or three, some with great wounds. And even those who came back with their bodies whole were changed in other ways. A neighbor of ours, the young Thomas Andrew, was home for weeks but sat silently all day before his house, unwilling to move from his chair. Sometimes as I ran by his house on some errand for my father, I would cry out to him heartily, "Good day to you, Thomas!" as if by shouting I could somehow rouse him from his wakeful slumber. But only his eyes moved in response, following me as I approached, passed, and left him behind.

Others returned home with tales of English triumph and their own valor. Jonathan Fisk showed anyone who listened how he had killed three Indians with his knife after his musket failed him. He acted out the drama with great enthusiasm. But showing us how he won this skirmish was not easy, because a bullet had wounded his right arm and now it dangled, shriveled and useless, by his side. Each of these men were heroes to those of us who were forced by our age or our sex to stay behind.

Yet when I heard of all the hundreds of Indian warriors who had been killed, I could not help but think of James. We had not received another letter from him and could not be sure he was still safe at Okommakamesit. Father often said he feared that all the Indians might soon be drawn into battle against us. And so I worried that James and Sam might one day aim their muskets against one another.

"Why so gloomy, Bartholomew?" my father asked as he took his turn at the press so that Annie might take a drink of sweetened cider. "This war will be over soon, and your brother home again."

"And what of James?" I asked.

My father now did not look so certain, but in the same cheerful way of his, he said, "James, too, will be back with us before long." The smile fled from his face, replaced by an angry determination. "I did not spend so much on his apprenticeship to lose the best printer in all of New England."

Yet I knew there was a greater cost to losing James than could be measured in pounds and shillings. My father missed his craftsmanship, his ability to set a straight line quickly, and sew a fine binding. But Annie and I missed his gentle nature and his good companionship.

One morning in late August, Sam came home, walking in the door of the printing shop as if he were returning from delivering books to Master Usher's shop across the river. Annie rushed up to him and threw her arms about his neck, grappling him so hard that he might have toppled to the earth if she did not release him. When I, more timidly, approached him, he surprised me by taking me up in his arms and spinning me about. He had never treated me before with such boisterous affection. I knew then that the war had changed him.

Father declared a day of thanksgiving. And for all the rest of that afternoon and into night, we did not one more jot of work, leaving the press just as it was, halfway through the printing of a proclamation. My mother roasted two fat geese and a dozen chickens, turning them upon spits set high in the fireplace so that their sweet aroma filled the house all the day. We celebrated into the evening, with neighbors joining in our festivities. There was plenty to eat, even for the children, and much cider and ale for all. It was a rowdy feast, and we only stopped for prayer three times, so large was our joy at Sam's homecoming.

My father was happier than Sam himself. "The work we'll do now that he's home!" Father said. "The commissions that he will bring us!"

But at first, Sam proved a disappointment. He was robust of body but not of mind, and given to idleness and ale. "What I have seen!" he told Goody Gray when she came by one evening with her buckets of cider. "I dare not tell you what I have seen!"

"Did you see any scalpings?" asked cousin Annie.

"Scalpings," Sam said, "and much worse. I cannot tell you all that I have seen." With our questions, Sam grew very serious.

"Were the Indians all terrible and frightening?" I asked him innocently.

He looked at me mournfully. "Yes, terrible. Yes, frightening," he said. "But ask me not about the Englishmen. About them, I will say nothing."

And for all those first weeks, as he sat idly in our printing shop as others worked about him, he was cheerful enough, but refused all talk about his many battles.

The month of August in the year 1675 ended with a terrible storm, which was called by some a furicane or a hurricano. Great winds came from the sea, pulling up whole trees as if they were but weeds plucked from a garden. The winds threw great ships up against the land and carried such a great downpouring of rain and hail that many crops were ruined and cattle swept away in sudden torrents.

At dinner, my mother complained that the vegetables she grew on a plot behind our house were destroyed. "I do not know how we will feed ourselves through the winter. These storms and the war, surely God has turned upon the people of New England," she said. "We have brought this upon ourselves with our wigs and fancy dresses."

"And the ribbons and the sweet scents and even dancing!" exploded my father. "Surely, the storm is punishment for our sins."

My brother Sam smiled at them. "Does not the same wind and the same rain strike our enemy?" he asked. "Perhaps the Almighty aimed His anger at them and missed His mark by a little."

Annie laughed and clapped her hands at this. Sam winked at her, as if there were a conspiracy between them.

Father looked at the two of them as he spoke to my mother. "Add to the errors of our day, that children no longer show their elders the respect that is due them."

But Sam spoke up. "If sins caused rain, then we would all be drowned," he said, "English and Indian alike."

I wanted to say that we should be happy that nearly all of us were safe and sound in a time of calamity. If only James were back with us! That night I prayed that he would return to us unharmed. Yet I did not expect my prayers to be quickly answered.

The next morning we were hard at work printing up a sermon for Annie's father, who was expected to visit us soon from Deerfield. Annie was not with us this day, but instead was helping my mother in the house. So it was that Sam helped my father and me and took his turn at the press. I marveled at how easily he was able to work the machine as we pressed out our pages one after the other, the ink black and gleaming upon the milky white of the paper.

It was not yet noon when we heard the steady booming of a drum. And then the church bell rang out, filling the town with its clangorous music. Sam rushed out of the shop and my father and I followed, racing to the beat of bell and drum.

Near the meetinghouse, we caught our first sight of them, a bedraggled little army of men walking in the heat upon the muddy road. Captain Moseley led the way, the only one riding upon a horse, which splashed mud upon all those who followed. Among them were twenty soldiers, a few in armored vests and helmets, and the rest in tattered clothing. Half carried muskets, the other half long pikes or swords, but all marched to the beat of the drummer, who followed behind them. Of all the soldiers, he was the best clad, his clothing somehow un-soiled. But under the summer's noon sun, he sweated as he banged out the rhythm on a huge kettle of an instrument that hung by a strap from his neck.

In the middle of this group were eight pris-oners, a chain of men tethered by ropes that they wore about their necks. Their clothes were English, made of sad-colored cloth. But their heads were bare as were their feet. They were Indians in English clothes. And they, too, stepped to the clockwork beating of the drum. The street was lined with townspeople now, all watching this sorry parade of disheveled men. Yet there was great cheering. Men doffed their hats, and some threw them in the air. Young children squealed, while their elders shouted out huzzahs and hoorays. So must it have been when Julius Caesar returned to Rome with his captives in chains behind him. A crowd is thrilled at the sight of a conquering hero.

Yet there was nothing splendid in Captain Moseley's troop of men and nothing fearsome in his captives. When I reached the avenue I could see that their skin bled from the rubbing of the rough rope that tied them neck to neck, more like goats to market than men.

The prisoners walked with their heads down, from shame or the weight of the ropes that held them. One was much taller than the rest, a Goliath of a man, his legs like tree trunks. People shouted out that they knew him, that he was called Little John. Yet I did not stare at him for long because I thought I knew another one of them, walking at the end of the line. I ran along the side of the road to get a better look at him. Like the others, he was filthy, as if he had been made to roll about on the muddy earth. He was the sorriest of sights, but, yes, I knew him. His hair, which he had once worn neatly in the manner of a Puritan gentleman, had been cut down to an uneven stubble, like a field of hay that had been mowed with a scythe. Worse still was the sad look upon his muddy face, so forlorn that I thought at any moment he could burst into crying. My heart felt as if it had fallen in my chest, a heavy stone.

"James," I said, so softly that it is a wonder he did hear me, "can it be you, James?" This bent and muddy man turned his head and fixed his gaze upon me. In his eyes, I saw a spark, a flame, an anger. Yet I paid that no attention, for now I was sure that this was he, my friend and my teacher. "It's James!" I shouted, jubilant to know that he was here among us with his head still upon his neck and not mounted on a pole. I ran to him, ready to rescue and claim him back, for surely he did not belong here among these ugly and broken men.

Captain Moseley whirled his horse about and trotted toward me. He could have no choice now but to release him, and all would be as it had been before, with James working at the press.

James called out to me, his voice cracking like a crow's caw. "Back away," he said. "You do not know me."

I wondered if he meant to shun me. For, of course, I did know him, and I would not back away. I heard the heavy thwack of the blow across my shoulder before I felt the pain. I turned to see Captain Moseley still upon his horse, a cudgel in his hand, ready to strike again. His face was drawn tight in a toothy smile, his blue eyes wild with rage.

"You would strike a boy, Moseley?" It was my father stepping in the road in front of me, placing himself squarely between me and Captain Moseley's horse. My father, as I have said, was a man of stout and hearty build, but he looked small before the captain on horseback. "You ride through town, sir, like a victorious general. But who have you brought here but simple men, who mean us no harm. I know some of them and they are praying Indians, who would not strike a blow against the English. One of them is my own apprentice, a hard worker and as good and honorable a man as lives in New England." Captain Moseley did not lower his arm. "I have my rights in this," my father said. "He's been apprenticed to me these many years."

Moseley stared in wonder at my father. And then he looked at the crowd that lined the road. All movement was suspended. Children who had picked up pebbles and rocks to throw at the prisoners held back their hands. Jeering men and cheering women were suddenly silent. The drummer ceased his beating. The church bell did not stop, but continued in its joyful ringing. All watched my father, who stood firmly in the path of the cruel captain.

Moseley clucked his horse forward. The animal took two steps and balked at going farther, his warm breath in my father's face. "You will not obstruct me, sir!" Captain Moseley said. "These are my prisoners. They may wear English clothes and play at being Christians for their own cunning purposes, but they are enemies all the same. And I take them to the governor. You must stand away!"

"I will not move, Captain," my father said. "I know what awaits them in Boston and I cannot let you feed their innocent blood to satisfy the hunger of the mob."

"Then you be damned!" Moseley said. "Forward!" he shouted to his troops. He gave his horse a vicious kick and rode straight ahead, knocking my father to the muddy ground.

It was then that I understood what my father already knew. James might be hanged, even though he was guilty of no offense.

"Drummer!" the captain shouted. Suddenly, the drummer began rapping out his beat again, a fast cadence that made my heart rush to keep up with it.

I ran to my father to help him to his feet,

while the troops and their prisoners walked swiftly to the bridge that would take them to Boston.

Our good neighbor Master Daniel Gookin stood by us. Gookin looked my father over and checked his scrapes and bruises. He tested my father's limbs with his thick hands and fingers. "You are muddied, Master Green, but unbroken," he said. "At least we can be thankful for that. But we can all see what has come to pass. Many Indians who have stood by us in this terrible war will trust us no longer. If we treat our friends in this way, we will turn every one of them against us."

Clambering to his feet, my father agreed. "We must go to the governor and his council to see that Captain Moseley does no harm to these poor men," my father said. "They must know the value of my apprentice."

"I worry about the mob more than Moseley," said Gookin. "Our fellow Englishmen have developed a taste for revenge. And they have a weak eye and a poor memory for faces. All Indians have come to look alike to them. But our good governor, Master John Leverett, still has the sense to know one from the other. And he will listen to you and me."

I was told to help Sam ready our two horses, while my mother put together food for the journey. In the stable, my brother was even more outraged than my father by what he had seen. "Has it come to this, that honest men must be roped together and led through the streets like cattle?" he asked. Before I could answer, he said, "And then to see a respected tradesman like our father, knocked to the ground as if he were a felonious criminal! This vexes me greatly, and the governor will hear my opinion of it!"

He led the horses to the house. My father and Master Gookin mounted up and were soon nicely settled upon horseback. Sam jumped up behind my father on our poor old mare, who strained against the weight of them as they rode away. By the time the travelers turned upon Wood Street, the horses had reached a steady trot.

Now Annie came running from the house, followed by my mother.

I asked Annie, "Do you think they will be able to save our James?"

"We can only pray and hope," Annie said. Whatever she believed would happen, she did not cry, and I took heart in this.

My mother bid us both to go to the shop and to finish what work we could this day.

"If you keep busy, you will not worry so much as if you were idle," she said. But it was not so, even though there was much labor left undone. As we began sorting type, the work seemed more difficult than it had that morning. We toiled through much of the afternoon in silence. When we finally stopped to ready ourselves for supper, I thought I could hear distant bells pealing out their welcome to Captain Moseley and his men. Annie wiped away the ink from her face and hands. And suddenly she had an inspiration. For the first time, she broke into an enormous, crooked smile. "We must go to Boston, to help save James. If we leave now, we can be there not long after dark."

"Father will be angry," I said.

"Not if we save James," Annie said. "Then he will forgive us."

"It is true," I said. "But my mother will not allow it, and it would be a sin to disobey her."

"If we do not ask, we need not disobey," said my cousin. I looked at her now with a new appreciation. She seemed to have ideas that were all her own, as if she were a child no longer. We packed up what bread there was in the shop and a bit of cheese, wrapping them in spoiled paper from the press. And by foot, we set off for Boston, taking a roundabout way so that no one would see us. The only one who did was young Master Thomas Andrew, who followed us only with his eyes. "Wish us well, Thomas!" I shouted. "We are off to save James Printer!" But Thomas kept his silence.

CHAPTER SIX

THE NOOSE

I᷐T WAS LONG DARK BY THE TIME WE REACHED Boston. Yet the streets were bright from a multitude of torches, and it seemed that few in the city were at home that night, long past the hour of curfew. There was a stream of them, men and women and children, all flowing in one direction with a single purpose.

"Hurrah for Captain Moseley!" said a little boy, a dark-haired urchin, grimy and with a terrible sore or growth upon one cheek. Small as he was, he held a smoking torch in a soot-blackened hand.

"Death to the savages!" answered another boy, this one taller and better cared for. "Death to the savages!"

The warm evening air was heavy with insects that circled about the flames the boys carried.

"Death to the savages!" the boys cried out together, and soon the crowd took up the cry.

"These foolish folks are the only savages I see," Annie said. "I worry that there is no kindness and courtesy left in this city."

She grabbed hold of my sleeve as we followed this meandering stream of people through the bent and winding streets. As the crowd grew thicker, she took my hand and I did cling to hers with all my might to keep from being separated. More than once, the moving mob congealed into a clot. Unable to stop, the people pressed ahead so hard that I easily could have been trampled, and Annie, too, if we were not careful to stay upon our feet. With all the smoke and flames, the jubilant anger of the crowd, I was glad to have Annie's hand in mine.

The moving crush stopped at the jailhouse, where the mob was chanting, "Death to the savages!" over and over to the beating of a military drum. A dark, heavyset man stood out front of the broad door. We soon learned that this was Captain James Oliver, the keeper of the jail. His face was strangely composed, one side of it drooping, his mouth in an odd half-smile. In one hand he held a cane, which he leaned upon.

Annie and I found a place to stand in a doorway at the top of a short run of stone steps, where we would not be squeezed by the crowd. We searched for my father, for Sam, for Master Gookin, but could not see them here.

Suddenly, someone shouted from the crowd, "Let us have them, Jimmy! Give us what is ours!" It was a man with an eye patch, the same Lemuel Brown I had seen in a tavern so many weeks before. I was not surprised to see him here, leading a mob. About him were men with ropes held in their hands or thrown over their shoulders.

I did not know from the look of Captain Oliver with his drooping half-face if he could change his expression if he wished, but he did not do so. "These men will have justice, Lemuel Brown," he said. His voice was not the loudest, but everyone could hear the force that was behind it. "They may be savages, but they have a right to English law."

"The outcome will be the same," replied Lemuel Brown. "Save yourself the trouble, Jimmy! Give them up." Others took up the cry. "Give them up! Give them up!"

Captain Oliver took one step into the crowd toward Lemuel Brown. He raised his cane and slapped it against his open hand. Snap. Snap. Snap. All other noise stopped, but for the insects singeing their wings in the torches.

"Most of you here know me. I am Captain James Oliver of the Boston militia, charged by Captain Samuel Moseley to keep these men in safety. What justice will finally bring to them, I cannot say. But keep them in safety is what I mean to do!"

"We'll give them justice ourselves upon the commons," said Lemuel Brown. I could see him clearly now in the light of the torches. His hair was dark and had been pulled out in odd places. There were sores on his cheeks, giving him a fearful look. Yet most frightening was not his appearance but that he now held in his hands a long coil of rope and had already fashioned a noose at its end.

"I can see what your verdict will be," Captain Oliver said. "Yet these men swear upon a Bible that they are God-fearing and never have made war upon the English."

"But I saw one of them myself at Brookfield, with my one good eye," said Lemuel Brown. "And it saw who killed our good Captain Hutchinson. It saw the one who struck him down without mercy."

Everyone in all of New England knew of the gallant Captain Hutchinson, who was killed at the battle of Brookfield a month before.

"And who is it you saw do the killing?" Captain Oliver asked.

"The enormous one, the one who is called 'Little John.' Let us have him tonight and we will trouble you no more, Captain."

The crowd was utterly silent as it waited for Captain Oliver's answer.

"Annie," I whispered, "he will not give him up, will he?"

But she did not reply.

Captain Oliver again raised his cane. Now

he shouted with a roar, "Go home! All of you, go home!"

But Lemuel Brown did not step back. And because he did not move, no one else moved, either.

And then with the suddenness of lightning, Captain Oliver struck Lemuel Brown across the face with the full force of his cane. Then wildly, he began turning in every direction, striking at the crowd over and over with all the fury of combat. It did not matter to him who was in his way, whether they be men or women or children. Because his anger was so much greater than all of the others' together, the mob moved back as if a whole battalion had attacked it.

And with some difficulty, because there was such a knot of humans assembled, the crowd turned in flight. Other soldiers now joined Captain Oliver, using clubs and muskets to push and jab the people of Boston away from the jail. Even Annie and I, who at first felt safe atop the little stairway, were routed out and forced to flee. How we escaped a beating I know not, but we ran as quickly as we could, following a trail of torches that set sparks flying like fireflies upon the air.

We ran far before we stopped, breathless, on a strange Boston street, unsure of where we were. It was then I caught sight of Lemuel Brown and some others, still carrying their ropes. They entered the tavern with the sign of the three boars. Master Usher's shop could not be far. And yet along the crooked paths and alleyways of Boston, we soon were lost.

"You be lost?" A boy of half my size came out of an alleyway, carrying a torch that filled the air with more soot than light. This was the same boy we had seen earlier, the one with a growth upon his cheek. Now that he stood still before us, I could see how poorly dressed he was, without a proper coat and hat.

"Lost we seem to be," Annie said.

"For a sixpence, I can help you find whoever it is you seek," the boy said.

"But we have not a penny with us," Annie said. "It would be a kindness if you could help us find my uncle and my cousin, who have come here to meet the governor."

"I know not who your uncle and cousin be, but as for the governor, he sits with the magistrates at the meetinghouse."

"Where is the meetinghouse?" I asked impatiently.

"You stand before it," the boy said. "But you won't get in unless you know a backward way. For the promise of a penny, I will show you."

"Then you have our promise," Annie said.

He led us down a dark alley that turned a sharp corner. Here he showed us where a window was left open in the summer's heat. "Through there and up the stairs," he said. "And for my penny, you can find me at the sign of the three boars."

He ran off in a shower of sparks from his torch. Now we stood in darkness. How still and warm was that night. Yet I shivered to think of that mob outside the jailhouse. Annie pulled herself up and through the window, and I was too frightened not to follow. Above us, up a flight of stairs, we could see the flickering glow of lamplight. And we were drawn to it the way the moths and insects fly into flame. We stepped slowly and carefully. But with each step, the boards of the stairway groaned with our weight. At the top was a brief corridor that quickly led to the open door of a large room, where men sat about a table in loud debate. No one noticed Annie and me, any more than if a pair of household cats had crept into the room and curled up in a corner.

I heard my father before I saw him.

"You, sir, know not the value of the man," he said. "You buy your rope by the shilling, but I measure this printer by the pound. If he is harmed, sir, there will be an accounting! An accounting! How many meals went into him, sir! Think of the flock of chickens, sir, devoured with a year's harvest of squash and beans and corn! Think only of the cheese, sir! A cartload of cheese has gone into him in all these years! And that is nothing to the expense of putting clothes upon his back! Harm him, and you will answer to me, sir!" He pounded the table. "You will answer to me!"

There was a mixed roar of anger and approval from the others. From where we stood, just outside the doorway, we could see my brother, his chair pushed out and his head tilted back as if there were a map upon the ceiling and he was studying it. Next to him sat good Master Gookin, his face flushed and puffed out with the words that he was ready to speak at any moment. And by his side was a man I had seen often in our village, Master John Eliot, the same man who removed James from his family and delivered him to the president of Harvard so many years before. Eliot was the author of the Indian Bible printed in my father's shop. His face was like no other I have ever seen, long and with a proud beak of a nose. There seemed to be no place for laughter in that face, and yet I saw that there was kindness in it. He was dressed all in black, as ministers always were in those days. His hair was long and white against the black cloth of his jacket. He looked down upon his hands now, as if he were in prayer or else half-asleep.

At the head of them all was Governor John Leverett himself. He was a handsome man, his hair still dark and straight. Like Eliot he dressed in black, with a white collar. There was no frill to his clothing this night, no splash of color like the red cape I once saw him wearing. Upon his head he wore a small skullcap. He thumped the table with a fist and asked for order. "Behave like the Englishmen you are and not the savages we fight!" he commanded. "Captain Moseley, what say you?"

Opposite my father, I saw the cruel figure of Captain Moseley. He rose to his feet. "Your honors, we came upon these men in an open field near the town of Marlborough, and they did turn and run. You know of the troubles that the English have there with these Indians. Thievery and worse. Storage sheds filled with grain that were burned to the ground. A cow cut loose from his owner's field and found some miles away, slaughtered. You talk of accounting. What price for this mischief? So when we saw these mischief makers run away, we did give chase for we knew we had found the guilty parties!"

Master Gookin now rose to his feet, much agitated, his hands in motion every way as he spoke. "I know them all, every one, and they are Christian men, all eight. And they no more deserve to be swung from the scaffold than any of us seated at this table."

"But they ran, sir," Moseley said. "Do you doubt that they ran?"

"And would you not run, Captain Moseley, if you were in their place, a company of men with muskets and pikes marching upon you?" Master Gookin said. "Tell me this, were you once fired upon? Did they show you even one sign of resistance? Your honor, Governor Leverett, these are praying Indians. They have no quarrel with us. They are friends to the English, our staunchest allies in this war against the truly savage tribes."

Moseley began to shout now. "Did you not hear yourself this night, the charges of Lemuel Brown, who saw one of these praying Indians of yours, one Little John, fire the musket that killed our own Captain Hutchinson? Your arguments fall to pieces against this cannon fire of evidence."

"I know not this Lemuel Brown or what he saw," said Master Gookin softly. "But the others among these Indians swear that John was at home near Marlborough at the time of the Brookfield battle."

"They swear it upon their Indian Bibles, I suppose," Captain Moseley said. "What they say cannot be trusted."

Now the Reverend Master Eliot seemed to awake, shaking his white mane as he spoke. "I, too, know these men, as you do not, Captain Moseley. There is Master Green's apprentice, the printer James. I have known him since he was a boy. No more devout soul exists among us. All of them have forsaken their savage ways. And if we turn against them now, if we take these eight men and march them to the commons, and hang them by their necks, we will have no Indian allies in this war. And who could blame every praying Indian for joining force against us?"

Governor Leverett now raised his hand, palm out, a sign that he had heard enough. "I see both sides to this quarrel," he said. "I understand the fears. Everywhere there are Indians still among us. They are servants in our homes. They work upon our wharves. If these, too, were to rise up in rebellion, who among us would be safe? In times such as these, we must take care. And it is also true that many of these so-called praying Indians are no more than heathens in English dress. They mouth the words, but their souls remain lost."

Master Eliot began to rise to his feet, but Governor Leverett raised his hand again. "Sir, hear me out," the governor said. "I know that there is truth in what you say as well. In the war against the Pequots, many of the Indian people were one with the English. And if we are to defeat King Philip, we will need our Indian alliances to hold, even if the governor of Plymouth colony is determined to drag every Indian into battle against us.

"So this is my decision. We will treat all eight of these Indians as required under the laws of Massachusetts Bay. If there be only suspicion of treachery and no evidence of it, then we must let them go."

Now it was Captain Moseley's turn to object. "But your honor . . ."

Again the governor raised his hand and with a wave of it brought back order.

"However, we cannot ignore the evidence brought forth by Goodman Lemuel Brown against the Indian known as Little John. I cannot say whether or not Goodman Brown is mistaken. That is for a court of law to decide. And so, tomorrow noon, this Little John is to be brought before the good magistrate, Master Edward Tyng, who will hear the evidence from all sides. And we must abide, Englishman and Indian alike, by the judgment of his court."

"And what of James?" my father said. "What of my apprentice?"

"We will hold him and the others for a time, and if there are charges against them, then a court of law must put them to rest."

With that, the governor rose. I raced to my father's side, troubled by what I had seen.

"Will he be hanged, Father?" I asked him. "Will James be hanged?"

Annie cried out, "You will stop them, won't you, Uncle?"

My father scowled. All thought of James seemed to be struck from his mind. "How did you come here? Have you disobeyed me?"

"We were afraid of what might become of James," I said.

"You should be worried more about the punishment due the souls of children who so freely disobey their parents," my father said, staring at me as if he were weighing the worth of my soul.

Annie came to our defense. "It is out of kindness we came," she said, "just as you have come."

My father paused. He rocked back and forth on his feet for several moments before he announced his conclusion. "You two shall stay the night with me at Master Eliot's house. And you will stand by me in court tomorrow to hear the arguments for Little John. I cannot say whether our James will be hanged or not, but you will know the outcome soon as I."

My father arranged to send a message home to my mother. "However good your intentions," he said to us, "you have brought great worry to that good lady. You will have to do much to earn her forgiveness."

We found our horses, which were stabled nearby. Master Gookin lifted Annie and me upon the back of one, and he led us down the Boston streets, which were quiet now except for the hollow beat of hoof on cobblestone. The old mare followed with Master Eliot upon her bowed back. My father and the others walked in silence all the way to Master Eliot's house in Roxbury. My brother and I were given a small bed to share, and all night long I did not sleep while Sam snored in my ears. Next morning, after a hasty breakfast, all of us walked back to the meetinghouse, where the trial was to take place. There was much talking now of who would speak first in defense of Little John.

Outside the meetinghouse, upon a post near the entrance where all were sure to see, someone had nailed a notice in an unpracticed hand. The writing said that "Guggins," meaning Master Gookin, was "a traitor to his king and country" and that this "Guggins" should "prepare for death."

Master Gookin tore down the sign, ripping it into fine pieces, which he cast into the street. "They who wrote this do not even have the courage to sign it! They sign themselves 'the New Society A.B.C.D.' When I know their names I will find them and thrash them just as I would a pack of pesky dogs."

"Take care," said Master Eliot. "Great fear brings even good men to do evil. Let us hope that this trial today can take that fear away."

But how gloomy all these wise old men looked to me that morning. And gloomy I must have looked as well, so fearful was I for James and the others. Only Annie smiled, taking pleasure in the sun of a new day. "Oh, I am not afraid," she said. "The truth is with us."

Already the meetinghouse was filling up. And as we walked in, many jeered at us, pointing and shouting out the names of us they knew. They singled out Master Gookin especially, calling him all manner of foul thing.

One tall boy in the crowd pointed at me and made frightful faces, putting his hands around his own neck as if he were choking me. I turned away, but he shouted, "Do not turn your head from me, for I know you, printer's brat!" he said. "The hangman waits for you, boy!"

"We've rope enough for all of them," said a man beside him in a raspy voice. "Indians and Indian lovers, all."

Annie took up my hand. "Do not fear these vile words, cousin, for they can do us no harm."

We found our seats near the front of the room, away from the angry rabble that filled the back. Still they shouted at us, and I turned to see the small boy who had guided us to Governor Leverett and my father the night before. He yawned now, after his late night. I thought that he must have earned the sixpence he was seeking, or even a shilling, by spreading word of the trial through the streets of Boston this morning.

Annie saw the boy, too.

"Have you the loan of a penny, cousin Sam?" she asked.

"What would you have with a penny?" my brother asked.

"Bartholomew and I have a debt to repay," she said.

Sam pulled out his money purse and found a full penny for her. When she stood up, all the jeering from the back of the meetinghouse was aimed at her, but it did not discourage her from her purpose. Slowly she made her way through the crowded aisles, with me following close behind, to the small, dirty boy. She handed him the penny.

"We make good our promises," she said.

"You are a kindly lady," said the boy, "and a brave one."

And as we walked back to the front, all the jeering stopped and a silence settled over the room.

When Captain Moseley entered, the crowd did rise all of a sudden to its feet to clap and cheer him. "Drunken babblers," I heard my father say. The captain did not wave or signal the mob, but upon hearing the roar of approval, he became ramrod straight, and I believe a small smile curled itself about his mouth. He pointed into the room and I followed the line of his finger to the place where I saw that Lemuel Brown now sat, his collar open, his face unshaven. Packed into a gallery of onlookers, Brown rose and slipped his body through the crowd. Captain Moseley bent down to speak to him, his mouth close by Brown's ear so that no one else would know what ideas he might be planting.

Just then Captain James Oliver hobbled in upon his cane. For a moment, the room was hushed and all could hear the rhythm of foot followed by cane, foot by cane. Then the gathering erupted into a volcano of jeering that was worse than was aimed at Master Gookin before. Still, Captain Oliver walked forward, his jaw set, his head as high as Captain Moseley's. When he reached the front of the room, he thumped his cane three times upon the wooden floor. "There will be order, or I will clear this court!" he said. And silence came upon the assembly with the suddenness of a summer rain. "Now bring in the prisoner!" he commanded.

Six men came in leading poor Little John. He had ropes about his neck and trunk, his hands were tied behind his back, and his feet were shackled together by chains so that he could only walk in small quick steps. To me, he seemed frightened, as if he had been crying.

And who could blame him? I knew in my heart that this large man, with a body like a bull's, was as meek in spirit as a lamb. The crowd soon began to shout terrible things at him. There were catcalls and much spitting. And some began throwing rotten fruit and worse. Little John was quickly covered and dripping with foul stuff, helpless to protect himself. Then Captain Oliver thumped his cane again, and all was still.

Now that Little John stood before us, I saw he had a large, misshapen jaw, and teeth that his lips could not keep covered. His arms were as large around as any blacksmith's. Yet, he was not much past being a boy, and was almost weeping.

Suddenly, a door was thrown open at the back of the room and a little, withered man walked briskly forward up an aisle that was partly blocked by onlookers. This was Master Tyng, the judge, and all rose to their feet and made way for him. When he reached the front, he wheeled quickly around and ordered us all, "Be seated!" And as if he were our schoolmaster, or the King of England himself, we all obeyed. He was old, even ancient, with hollow cheeks and a mouth so puckered, it looked like a piece of fruit, split open and dried in the sun. And he shook as he spoke, shivering as if it were not the hottest day of September but winter, and he had stayed out too long in the cold. But forget what a little man he was. Today he stood not alone, but as the entire colony of Massachusetts Bay. In a single sentence, written down on paper and signed in his own hand, he could set a man free or send him to the gallows.

"Where is the prisoner?" he asked. I thought the judge must be the only man in the room who did not know. Who else but this giant of a man, tethered by ropes, surrounded by guardians, could be the prisoner?

"He stands before you, here," said Captain Moseley.

"How is he charged?" asked the judge.

Captain Moseley read the charges from a piece of paper he held before him. The list was long. But the final one was the most important. "This Little John," Captain Moseley read, "did brutally and for no cause strike down Captain Edward Hutchinson."

The crowd murmured, but Captain James Oliver's cane brought quiet.

"How say you, the accused?" the judge asked the Indian.

"I have done nothing," the man said. "As Christ be my witness, I am an innocent man. I have no quarrel with you English and have never taken arms against you." I wondered how anyone could doubt this gentle man's honesty.

But the crowd stamped and clapped and whistled. "He lies!" shouted Lemuel Brown, who now rose from his seat and stepped up on a bench so that all could see and hear him. "I saw the deed myself. He brought up his musket and fired upon Captain Hutchinson. Shot him in the back of his head!" Now the others around him began screaming oaths so terrible that I cannot write them out.

The judge did his best to shout for order. But only Captain Oliver with his cane was able to silence this mob. This allowed Judge Tyng to bring out a jury, which had not one Indian upon it.

Seeing this, Master Gookin rose up to object.

"Is it not the custom to have a jury of Indians

of good repute to pass judgment on one of their own?" he asked.

"In this case," said Judge Tyng, "that will not be necessary." He called up Lemuel Brown to say what he had seen at Brookfield a month before. He spoke not to the judge but to the spectators in the room. And he appeared to enjoy every terrible detail. "Oh, I was there," he said, "and with my one good eye did I see this Little John shoot down the poor, young Captain Hutchinson."

The crowd moaned.

"And then with the same eye did I see this Little John cut off the head of Captain Hutchinson as the poor soldier lay bleeding in the field."

Master Gookin jumped to his feet. "This is a lie, sir! A lie! The late lamented captain's head never left his wounded body. It was buried with him. And it is well known that Captain Hutchinson did not die at once from his wounds but some days after the battle. This is a made-up tale."

"I may be wrong in some of the details," said Lemuel Brown, smiling now, "but I know that I saw this Indian before me fire his musket and bring down a fine young Englishman."

The crowd was impatient. "The verdict's plain!" one man shouted. "Hang the Indian!" yelled another.

But Master Gookin, still standing, turned around the room and addressed the crowd himself. "Does the truth not matter here? Does it not matter that others of his tribe say he never traveled to Brookfield at all, but was at Marlborough, a day's journey away?"

"You'd take a heathen's word over my own?" asked Lemuel Brown.

"No! No!" answered the spectators.

"This is for the jury to decide," said the judge.

The members of the jury left the room, but took little time in returning. The verdict was what I feared most. The jurors found Little John guilty. The crowd roared its pleasure. The judge calmed them so he could pronounce the sentence. The Indian known as Little John, he said, was to be hanged this very morning upon the commons.

Now the crowd did celebrate, dancing and clapping, shouting and singing. It was as if sending this sad giant to his death brought a victory over the dreaded King Philip.

"But, Father," I said. "This man did none of what he was accused. How can he be hanged?"

"I think you are right in that, Bartholomew," he said. "The Indian is innocent, but it is the jury's case to decide, not yours or mine."

"And now is James to die, too?" I asked.

"Master Gookin and I will work for his release. He is innocent of wrong, of that I am sure. But from what I see today, this mob is hungry and must be fed. How large an appetite it has, I know not."

I turned to see Annie, clinging to Master Eliot, crying.

We waited until the room emptied to push outside, where there was a huge crowd waiting, as large as the one outside the jail the night before. They followed Captain Oliver and the armed men who surrounded Little John. The air was full of wild taunts and ugly cries. It was strange that the sun shone down as on any summer's day, warm and bright, calling the children of Boston to play and swim in the long hours before night.

I saw Master Eliot push ahead through the crowd and reach the prisoner. He put a hand upon Captain Oliver's shoulder and spoke into the soldier's ear. I could not hear what was said, but afterward, Master Eliot was allowed to walk by Little John's side as we all marched toward the commons. There, I saw a high platform, so newly made that I could smell the sweetness of the raw wood even at some distance. The Indian named Little John walked up the steps with Master Eliot. The crowd was noisy all the time, even when Little John and Master Eliot kneeled together in prayer. "Before God, I am innocent," the Indian said, and with such force and honesty that the crowd grew still. For the first time this day, the mob had doubts. But then Captain Oliver stood beside the kneeling Little John and ordered him to his feet. He put a noose about the condemned man's neck, placing it there gently as if it were a necklace. "This is my sad duty, for I believe you are innocent," Captain Oliver said. "Please have no hatred for me."

"I hate you not," said Little John.

From the hushed crowd, Captain Moseley came forward and shouted, "Be done with it."

I saw that the slack rope ran over a high rounded beam and then down to three men of

Captain Oliver's company, who held the end in their hands.

My knees were weak and I thought I would crumple to the ground. My father seeing this said to me, "Be brave, Bartholomew. A man must know the world."

Pale as paper, Annie stood tall and tearless beside me. "You can look away," she whispered.

But I could not. My eyes were fixed on this gentle Indian who stood before us so alive.

Then James Oliver said, "Now! Be done quickly!" And the three men pulled upon the rope and hoisted Little John up into the air by his neck. But he was so heavy a burden that they could not hold him, and soon they let him fall to the ground. My stomach jumped up into my throat. And then they pulled again, and again he rose and fell to the platform with a heavy thump.

Once more Captain Oliver gave the order. But just then, an Indian in deerskin clothes leaped upon the platform and drew a knife. Before anyone could prevent it, he stabbed poor Little John in the chest. Blood burst from the wound like a fountain. And in no more than three heartbeats, the giant fell to the ground, dead.

I saw all this myself, as did many an English child on that afternoon upon the commons. And it was a terrible thing. I lost all that I had eaten. And I was not the only one who was made sick by what I saw.

We were to see many terrible events in the time of King Philip's war. But none was worse than this.

Later, there were many stories told about the strange Indian who took Little John's life. Some said that he did what he did because of the savage belief that if he drank the Indian's blood, the dead man's spirit and strength would enter his own body. But this is a false report. It did not happen. Instead, I think, this second Indian took pity on Little John and acted to shorten his suffering. Whatever his reason, he somehow vanished into the crowd and was never seen again.

Within minutes, Little John's head was mounted upon a pole. I stared at his bruised and lifeless face. "It is best not to look," said Annie, too late. "It is intended to put fear into the hearts of evil men. But it was not meant to torment goodly souls like yours." Yet how could I not look?

Master Gookin was angry. "That head of Little John's will frighten even innocent men," he said. And I knew that he was right.

Yet when I looked upon the head of Little John, I knew that what I saw was not the man but a discarded piece of him. It was no more Little John than his worn-out shirt or a lock of his hair.

My cousin Annie, she of the cheerful face and happy spirit, was now as glum as anyone. For once, I was the one to comfort her. "It will be all right," I said.

"If you think so, Bartholomew," she said. But still her smile was gone.

Instead of going home straight away, we stayed in Boston a while longer, and my father sent word to my mother that we would spend a few nights more with Master Eliot. The next day, Father and Master Gookin gathered all who knew of James, and we paid a visit to Governor Leverett. His house was three stories high and topped with many little peaks, the grandest home in all of Boston.

The governor greeted us himself but offered little comfort.

"Dear friends," he said, his eyes turned away, his face somber. "I will do what I can for the Indian printer. But you must be patient with me." We returned to Master Eliot's house and waited.

And all the while, I imagined James in a cramped jail cell, not knowing if this day would be his very last on this earth.

The next night Master Gookin woke us from our troubled sleep. Sam stopped snoring, and we quickly rose and dressed. Set upon a horse together, Annie and I rode through the darkened streets, not knowing where we were going. I was still only awake by half when we came to the jail. There was no mob, and only a single torch burned outside the door where a man with a musket stood guard. "We've come to see Captain Oliver," Master Gookin said.

"He has been expecting you," said the man. He knocked upon the door and it opened. We all crowded our way into a small, airless room — Master Gookin, my father and brother, Annie and I. The only furniture was a plank table and two chairs. At the far end was a heavy door with a small window in it. Captain Oliver took Master Gookin's hand in his. "I'll get him," the captain said.

He opened the thick wooden door and a foul smell swept into the room, the scent of sweat and sickness and fear. We watched as the captain walked down a dim corridor past another guard, with his cane in one hand and a ring of keys in the other. He unlocked a door and disappeared into a room.

When he came out again, he brought James with him. We surrounded our friend and greeted him with hearty handshakes and great embraces. I expected him to be glad and to smile, especially on Annie and me. But James said very little and seemed forlorn. He squinted in the lamplight. I saw that he was wearing clean English clothes and leather shoes upon his feet.

Captain Oliver said, "You may go now and wherever you please, James Printer. But I would not stay in Boston and I would chart my course clear of all cities and towns, for we have seen what my own countrymen can do when fright takes hold of them and throws out their better natures."

"I will stay far away," James said, and in his voice was more than sadness. "I have no longing to be in cities, no wish to be with people who hate and would harm me."

"Cannot James stay with us?" I asked. "We would let no harm come to him."

James turned to me and smiled kindly, just the way he would if I had set a crooked line of type or smeared the print upon a page. "There is no place I would rather be than in your shop, working upon your press, putting beautiful words on fine English paper. But the world has turned around, and it cannot be."

I was crying now, and Annie, too. He reached out to both of us and held us to him. And there we would have stood for hours, for days, if Captain Oliver did not open up the door and lead us into the night.

Outside the jail, my father gave James a sack of food to carry and a five-pound note. And Master Gookin gave him the hat from his head, a tall black hat that covered James's cropped hair and helped to hide his face.

"Go to Natick, James," said Master Gookin. "Or go to your father at Hassanamesitt. You will be safe in either place, at least for now."

"Will we see you again, James?" I asked.

James put his hand on my shoulder and squeezed it. "No man can know that, Bartholomew. For now, I must run to the west, as quickly and as far as I can go. There is safety nowhere else."

Annie leaned against him, and he gently stroked her hair. "When the war is over, we will look for you," she said.

"And if I am alive, you will find me," he said. But already he was looking to the west, probably trying to remember his way out of the city.

"You must fly, James," Master Gookin said. "Do not let the sun find you here."

James hesitated, looking at me among all the others, and said, "Do not believe all that you will hear of me."

He pulled the brim of his hat forward and walked quickly away, turning a corner and vanishing from our sight. For a moment, I wondered what horrors might be waiting him, and I could not bear the thought.

CHAPTER SEVEN

IN THE CAMP OF
KING PHILIP

FOUR DAYS LATER, ANNIE'S FATHER CAME TO take her to Deerfield. "It will be as safe there as it is in Cambridge," he told my mother. "We have a fine new house, with wooden floors of solid planks, and my good wife, who is frail of health and needs the help of a daughter, will hear no argument against Annie's coming home."

And so, within a week, I had lost James again, and now Annie was leaving, too. She took with her a small parcel of clothing, no more than she had brought. "She is a good and obedient child," my mother told my uncle, "and we will miss her." Before he came, I had heard my mother say that Annie would be safer with us than in the woods of the west, where wolves ran in packs and bears burst into people's houses. And most worrisome of all, she said, there were reports of rebel Indian attacks upon little settlements in the wilderness, where there were no regiments to guard them. But my mother did not say this to my Uncle Robert. He had made up his mind, and it was said of the Clarks that they did not easily part with their opinions.

As for my father, a tear was rolling down one cheek but not the other. It was as if he had two minds: one sad that Annie was going, the other glad that she would no longer be an expense. But he said only, "I am losing the dearest printer in all New England." And I knew that my father had no kinder words to say of anyone. Annie gave my mother and father each a sweet embrace and then Sam lifted her from the ground in the heartiness of his farewell.

As for me, I suddenly grew shy of my tall

and freckled cousin. I knew not what to say to her, my dearest companion. She spoke before I could. "I will miss you most of all, Bartholomew," she said. And my throat would not let me speak. But I think she could see the words I wanted to say as plainly as if they were printed upon my face, like a page in a book. She touched my head with a gentle hand, then left us and mounted her father's horse, sitting close behind him. In the time it takes to turn a page, they were gone.

How saddened was I? It was as if a part of me had been taken away, a hand or a foot. There was no time when I did not miss her pleasant face and cheerful smile, and suffer for my loss. But in a time of war, there were many leavings and much sadness. The cure for the ailment, my father said, was to work all the harder. "A mind left idle will wander into swamps, and there stay mired, never returning to happiness or light," he liked to say. Over and over and over. For he also liked to say that a lesson worth knowing was worth repeating. And so, to keep me from wandering into a bog of loneliness and grief, he gave me work to do that filled every moment of my days and left me too tired at night even for dreaming. At the end of each long day, I tumbled into sleep as if I were falling into a dark and bottomless well.

No word of my uncle and cousin did we hear for many days.

One night after supper, Goody Gray came to our shop, but without her usual cakes and ale and cider. "Master Green," she said to my father, "there's terrible news. The soldiers were evacuating the town of Deerfield when they ran into an ambuscade at Muddy Brook. They are calling it Bloody Brook today. All have perished! And those who have not perished are enslaved by the savages! A disaster!"

"Deerfield, Goodwife Gray! An ambush! Is it Deerfield, you say?"

"Deerfield it is," said the old woman. "The same Deerfield where your little Annie and her papa are gone to. Forgive me, Master Green, but it is my unhappy duty to tell you this."

"But all cannot be dead," I said.

"Not Annie! Surely not!" said Sam.

"All of them. Perished or captured," said the old woman. "And captured is the worse of the two, from what I know of savages."

"Calm yourself, good woman," my father

said. "There have been so many false reports."

"And many that are true," she replied.

For my part, I simply could not believe what she had said. Was it not just days ago when Annie left us? And this was no time of plague, where hearty persons such as she are struck down dead. "Dead," I found myself saying. "They cannot all be dead."

Just then, Master Gookin rushed into the shop. He saw the dreadful looks upon all of our faces, and Goody Gray was sobbing now. "You've heard, then, of Muddy Brook," he said.

"It's true, then?" Sam asked him. "That all are dead or captured?"

"Not all," said Master Gookin. "Not everyone. A few escaped. But a very few. And one of them is your mother's brother, Robert Clark. He was wounded, but not killed. That's why I have called on you this night. He asked to be taken here, and will arrive by morning."

"How grave are his injuries, pray that you tell me?" my father said.

"Very grave," Master Gookin said.

"And what of Annie?" I asked.

"And her dear mother?" my father asked.

"We do not know for certain," Master Gookin said. "But Master Clark thinks they were taken by the Indians."

"My wife must know all this at once," my father said. We quickly closed up the shop and all went to our house. None of us slept before morning.

When I saw my uncle, I wondered if he was the same man who I had last seen leaving us for Deerfield. He came upon horseback, not riding upright, but slung over the animal's back like a sack of grain. My mother pronounced him pale, but he was not so much pale as gray, like a stone in a churchyard.

He could scarcely talk, and when he could, he would moan. "King Philip's camp," he said. "Both are taken to King Philip's camp."

My mother took command of him, and all in the household were her troops. Nothing he wanted was denied him. No need of his was too great for us to meet. She fed him with the frantic care a mother robin pays upon her fledglings. And to our happy surprise, she brought him slowly back to life.

One evening in October, Master Gookin came to call on us, only to find my Uncle

Robert sitting in a chair in the warmth of our parlor.

"Master Gookin," my uncle said, with a voice hardly louder than a whisper, "you seem surprised to see me sitting here. Well, I am surprised myself to be here, for I thought I would sit no more, but lie instead for all eternity."

Master Gookin took his hand. "Sir, I confess surprise at this, a miracle."

"You came at a good moment," my uncle said, "for I begin to tell the story of Bloody Brook, now that I have the strength to tell it."

And so he told us of the days that followed his leaving Cambridge.

"Annie was so happy on that last of summer days, singing and laughing as we rode along toward Deerfield, under swaying willow and rustling aspen. But soon we came to a cluster of burned-out cabins, the beams still standing but charcoal black. Each was no longer a house but the charred skeleton of one. Across a clearing, the contents of a household were tossed and scattered as if by a wild animal. A mattress ripped and shredded. A clothes chest split open, and the clothing torn and tossed. A mirror shattered. A dead ox lay in the middle of the road. The war had come here just days before.

"As we neared Deerfield, I rode all the faster. And there the village sat, a score of little houses, beyond the war, as safe as when we left it. Or so it seemed, off in the distance.

"But as we neared our house, I was puzzled to see men and women and children upon the green, whole families loading their belongings into ox-drawn carts. Large numbers of soldiers with muskets and pikes stood at the edge of the green and on the road, watching over them.

"My dear Elizabeth rushed out to greet us. She told us that a Captain Lathrop had come to warn of a pending Indian attack, and that all must pack up their possessions and leave this place. So my homecoming proved to be a leave-taking. We moved what belongings we could onto one of the carts and set off to the east. How proud I was of my Annie, who with her strength helped me pile our things upon a pyramid of furniture and crates and mattresses.

"The day was so hot, I pitied the oxen. Captain Lathrop would not let us rest. A few miles away we came to a little brook winding through trees and meadows. Now that it was summer, the water was low, but still it slowed the caravan as one ox-drawn cart after another dipped and tilted across its banks.

"Our company was only partly across when I heard the first arrow, heard it before I saw it, a feathered stick singing through the breathless air. This was followed by a rain of arrows, a storm showering upon livestock and villagers and soldiers alike. The sound was like a strong wind shaking boughs of poplars. They came in gusts, hundreds of arrows and then hundreds more.

"Then there was a brief moment of quiet, unbroken by wind or weapon, voice or breath. Finally, a wounded ox moaned and was answered by a wounded man, the two sounding alike. Annie and Elizabeth still stood. But I sat upon the ground. How I arrived in this position I did not know. A feathered arrow stood out from my chest, like a branch from a tree. Annie helped me to my feet so that we might run, but we did not know which direction to take.

"Captain Lathrop himself walked by, the shaft of a broken arrow protruding from his back. He did try to speak with us, but when he opened his mouth, no words came forth, only the dark eloquence of his spilling blood.

"Then we heard the cries of the Indian warriors and the slaughter began again. They hunt animals with greater mercy. And soon the stream ran red with English blood, and I thought that soon we all must die.

"I saw an Indian running toward us. He was half-dressed in deerskin leggings, a great tomahawk in one hand, a long knife tethered to his belt. His face was painted red, with black lines on forehead, cheeks, and chin. One of his eyes was clouded over with a gray cast. And about his neck he wore a necklace of fingers, and my terror grew so great that I could make no sound, but only wait. As he came closer, I could even smell the rancid bear grease he used to coat his hair. He raised his arm and in his hand, I saw the great rounded stone at the head of his tomahawk that would shatter our skulls. I thought how quick it would be. Our souls would fly up, fearless, free of the earth, lighter than any bird.

"Then I heard someone cry, 'Stop! Hold your weapon!' This was an English voice. I turned my head to see an Indian dressed in English clothes, a tall man made even taller by a high hat that seemed too large for him. He walked without hurrying, as if he moved in a calm in which there was no battle and no war.

"'James,' I heard my Annie say, 'he will save us.' But he paid her no attention and spoke instead to the warrior, calling him One-Eyed John. They argued for a time in a tongue I did not understand.

"This One-Eyed John pushed Annie and Elizabeth toward James. He then grabbed hold of my hair and was ready to take away my scalp, when this same James stopped him once again. Though James's manner was gentle, the wild warrior meekly obeyed him, as if the one had a magical power over the other. 'Have no worries,' James said to me. 'I will look after your wife and your daughter.'

"They were taken as captives, five women, three girls, and two young boys, altogether, Annie and Elizabeth among them. They left without time for good-byes. A trapper found me two terrible days later, still sitting in a field of carnage, the only one left alive."

My Uncle Robert, weary now, could speak no more that night. Still, his words gave me all the reason to believe that Annie was alive, and James with her. I thought of Goody Gray's terrible words, that it was better to perish than be captured. But I did not believe that, for my cousin had James to protect her.

My uncle's improvement continued as the fall air turned sharply cold, promising a snowy winter. It was Sam's belief that the war would ease with the first icy storm or blizzard, but it did not. The Indians persisted in their frightful attacks upon outlying towns and settlements. Some of these, the Indians burned to the ground, while the settlers stayed within their houses for fear of being massacred.

One evening, not long after my family had finished a meager supper and my uncle was gone to bed, we heard a fierce knocking upon our door. At my father's bidding, I ran to open it, and there before me stood a large, hardy man, as round as any well-fed Englishman and as tall as any Indian.

Under a cloak of bear fur, he was dressed in leather leggings and leather shirt, and he wore a cap of mismatched skins—of skunk and fox, beaver and wolf. I might have thought him an Indian, except for his beard, which was brown and silver as if it had been touched by frost. In one hand, he held a musket, in the other, a thin rectangular object wrapped in deerskin.

Even before he said one word, I knew him to be the trapper and trader John Hoar, although I had never seen him before. My father had known him since they were both penniless young men, first landed from England, and I had heard much of the trapper's adventures.

"John Hoar," my father bellowed, walking up behind me. "Good man, do not stand there letting in a draft on a cool night."

The trapper took two steps forward and put his gun to rest against a wall as my father slammed the door behind him. Father then grabbed hold of the big man's shoulders and embraced him like a lost cousin come home again.

"Still alive, I'm glad to see," said my father, who bid me pour out two cups of Goody Gray's cider as he led John Hoar into our kitchen. The trapper warmed his frosted limbs by the fire. I thought he smelled like a wet horse.

"Alive to the displeasure of many, for there's many an Englishman I know who would see me dead," said Master Hoar, gulping down the warm cider, then holding up his cup so that I would pour him another. "For I trade with the Indians. And I do agree that I trade with them, taking what furs they give me for pots and kettles and good English currency. That is what I do for my living. And I ask those who say I should give it up, how am I to eat and drink if I have no livelihood? And if I do sometimes exchange liquor for furs, what of it? Don't I give value for value? I am an honest tradesman like yourself, Samuel Green, and must make my living how I can." He finished his second cup of cider and all of a sudden sat down in a chair by the hearth, his long legs stretched out so far before him that I thought his leggings might be cooked by the fire. My father pulled up a chair beside him.

"No one questions your honesty here in this house," my father said, smiling.

"There are many elsewhere who do, Samuel Green, so I thank you for that," the trapper said.

"What brings you to Cambridge on a cold evening such as this?" my father asked.

"I have tidings," said the trapper, who picked up the rectangular object he had been carrying and unwrapped it. It was a book, nothing more or less. "You must see what is recorded here in this ledger."

With great care he opened up the book and turned one leaf after another. I moved close behind him, standing between the two chairs, so I could view what was on these pages, and what I saw looked ordinary enough. It was here that Master Hoar kept his accounts.

"William White of Natick," said one entry. "Fourteen beaver furs, finest. Five fox, two finest, three of middle grade. Eighteen rabbits, mixed. One pound and eight shillings. One bottle, canary wine."

He did not linger, but instead continued turning until he came to pages that were different from the others, written in a finer hand, in looping letters that grew thin and thick as they ran their course.

"Here they are," said Master Hoar. "These are what you will want to see." He pointed a thumb toward the middle of the page and then handed the book to my father, who sat next to the trader. Standing between them, I was able to look over my father's shoulder as he read.

"Annah Clark of Deerfield, late of Cambridge," it said, in a fine hand. "Daughter of the Reverend Master Robert Clark, Deerfield. Five pounds English, or two flintlock muskets, small keg powder.

"Elizabeth Clark of Deerfield," said the next entry. "Wife to the Reverend Master Robert Clark, Deerfield. Twelve pounds English, or five flintlock muskets, two kegs powder."

"You have seen them?" my father asked. "Annie and her mother?"

"Seen them?" said the trapper. "Why, my good friend, I have supped with them, conversed with them, laughed and cried with them."

"And are they well?"

"As well as they might be, living as they are, hostages in King Philip's camp!"

"The numbers there, five English pounds and twelve pounds more," my father asked, "these are the ransoms that King Philip asks for their release?"

"Indeed, they are, sir. I have gotten these from King Philip himself."

"Well, seventeen pounds, that is a princely sum," said my father with a sigh. "Yet, I will help to raise this and more, to win their release, if I am permitted. You see, Governor Leverett has vowed to send not one gun or ounce of powder or penny to the rebel Indians in exchange for captives. He says that to do this is to purchase the death or capture of many more good English people. He would starve these rebel Indians out this winter and then defeat them in the spring.

"But, tell me, John," my father continued, "how did they seem to you, my niece and her mother?"

"They are well, but not as well as I would like," answered Master Hoar. "Food is scanty among the Indians. All within the camp, captives and Indians alike, are given a fair share. But it is too little, I think, and soon there will be less. Why, Mistress Clark told me herself that most of the grain was gone and game scarce. When a sickly horse died, it was divided up, hooves, hide, and all. There were some among the English who would not eat of horse, and if they died by this choice, the Indians did not care. But Mistress Clark said that she and Annie ate their portion and thought little of it."

Now Master Hoar rapped a finger upon the open book and said, "But you have not read all upon this page."

"Why, certainly I have. There are only two entries here and I have read them both," my father said.

"Look further there," demanded Master Hoar. "Do you not recognize this hand?"

I blurted out the answer. "Why, it's James's writing, is it not, Master Hoar?"

"Indeed, you are a bright penny of a boy," said the trapper. "For James was in King Philip's camp and acted as my scribe, taking down in his well-schooled hand the names of captives and the ransoms wanted."

"He is a traitor, then," said my father sadly. "And I have lost the benefit of my investment."

"I do not call him traitor, Samuel," said the trapper. "For he is guardian angel to all the English captives. And it is James who urges Philip to release them. Why, it was James who told me that the Indian king has a fondness for canary wine and might give them all their freedom for a dozen bottles of that or any other liquor."

"I knew it!" my father said, more cheerfully. "He protects them all! And when this war is done, as it will be soon, I will have my apprentice back again!"

The next morning early, after showing his ledger book again and telling his tale for the benefit of my mother and my Uncle Robert, Master Hoar was off to see Governor Leverett. "I will urge him to make an offer to King Philip to release his prisoners," he explained. "The amounts are small weighed against the value of a life."

Soon we learned that the governor did not want to change his policy. "The winter is a cannon in our war against these Indians," he told Master Hoar. "It would be foolish to give King Philip a shield against our strongest weapon."

We saw no more of Master Hoar that winter, and there was not another word of poor Annie and her mother.

All was black outside in late February, the ground still frozen, the snow falling heavily, when we had a visitor to our printing shop. It was so dark, even in the middle of the day, that we had to burn a full regiment of candles to make our almanac ready before the first of spring.

Our visitor flung open the door. It was Captain Samuel Moseley, his scowling face as frozen as the river Charles in midwinter.

My father gave him every courtesy. "Captain, come warm yourself," he said, and ladled up a cup of mulled cider. This warmed his hands and thawed his belly, but did nothing to melt his frozen face.

"I have come to show you something, Master Green," Captain Moseley said. "It was found just four days ago, nailed upon the bridge at Medfield after the slaughter of most who lived there."

The soldier took a paper from his coat and unfolded it for us to see.

My father read the sentences aloud. "'Know by this paper, that the Indians you have provoked to wrath and anger will war this twenty-one years, if you will. There are yet many Indians. We come three hundred at a time. You must consider the Indians lose nothing but their life. You must lose your fair houses and your cattle.' This is a terrible note, Captain. A most troubling note. Whoever in New England hears of it will be stoked into a flaming rage against our enemy."

"I agree with you, Master Green," said Captain Moseley, who seemed satisfied with my father's response. "What if I told you that upon the word of an Indian spy, I believe this paper to be the scribbling of your apprentice, James the printer? Would your rage now be directed against him?"

"No, sir. It would be directed against your spy," said my father. "For I have only contempt for liars, Captain."

"And what if I were to tell you that I have reason to believe that this writing *is* by your James, and that he is well known to dwell in King Philip's camp."

My father sighed. "If I knew these to be James's thoughts, then I would be amazed, Captain. I do not believe he has changed as much as this."

"Then please have a second look at it, sir, and tell me if you know the writing to be his," said the captain.

Captain Moseley laid the paper upon a table before my father. I could see it plainly, although it was smudged with soot and grease from much handling. While my father studied the writing, so did I, following the lines as they curved upon the page, from thick to thin and thick again, in the pleasant sweep of a well-schooled hand. I knew I had seen the hand-writing before.

Yet my father puzzled over it, holding the note before him, first at some distance and then close to his nose as if he would know the author by its scent. "I know James's hand, certainly I do," said my father. "And whether this be his hand or not, I cannot say."

Captain Moseley, who had been sitting with a half cup of cider, now jumped to his feet, all politeness and patience vanished like melted snow. "*Cannot* say, sir, or *will* not?"

"I read the words and know they are not his," my father said. "He is not a man to be filled with wrath, who might threaten English homes. This is his home, here with us. And here he would be if he had not been driven away!"

"I ask not about the words expressed but about the hand that wrote them," Moseley said. "Did your printer James write them or did he not?"

My father shook his head as he looked upon the paper. "That is the problem I have. First, the words are not his. That to me is certain. Words are but thoughts upon paper, and these words are no thoughts that James might have set down. As for the lettering, sir, sometimes I think these letters are his and sometimes I think they are not."

The captain snatched the paper from my father's hand and put it before my face.

"What say you, boy? Do you know this hand or not? Remember, if you are not truthful, your soul must lie in Hell for all eternity."

I thought of Hell, full of sorrow that never ends, and I thought of my friend, of his kindly dark eyes and gentle manner. Then I said, oh so softly, "I do not believe these letters were made by James."

Angrily, Captain Moseley folded up the note and tucked it in his coat pocket.

"Your souls be damned, father and son!" he said, walking for the door. "As for the hand that wrote this note, it will be chopped from its arm and delivered to the governor before I am finished." He slammed shut the door and was gone with great haste.

"If anyone cuts off that printer's hand," my father said, with the captain gone, "he will have to answer to me!"

I could imagine before me an image of poor James's severed hand. Then my thoughts turned to what Captain Moseley had said.

"Do you believe in a Heaven and a Hell, Father?" I asked him.

"Well, of course, I do," he answered. "What Christian does not believe?"

"Will I go to Hell, Father?" I asked.

"Why so?"

"For lying to Captain Moseley," I said. "For it is a sin to lie, just as he said."

"Captain Moseley knows not whether you spoke the truth, my dear Bartholomew."

"But I know it, Father, and I worry that I will be cast into Hell," I said.

Now my father smiled upon me, his face as welcome as a glorious sunrise upon a fine spring morning.

"Hell is not for you, my good young man," he said quietly. "And when you in your time reach the Gates of Heaven, it is my fondest hope that I will be there to greet you."

"And James," I asked, "will he be there, too?"

"Whatever his sins, however terrible, I think that they will be forgiven," he said.

"And Captain Moseley, will he be in Heaven?" I asked, not at all sure I wanted to go if he would be there.

My father frowned and in his loudest voice declared, "Not if he does any harm to my Indian apprentice!"

CHAPTER EIGHT

War's End

Because I was a printer's devil in my father's shop in that year of 1676, I knew every tragedy and triumph of King Philip's war. For each joyous victory and every sad defeat, there was a proclamation or a sermon to be printed. In the spring there were new massacres of English troops. The towns of Groton and Marlborough were destroyed in Indian attacks. Part of the city of Providence in Rhode Island was burned to the ground. And news of these events I often set into type by myself, my fingers slapping the little pieces of lead into place, line by line with a click-click that was now faster than my father's.

It seemed there was no place that was safe, not even Cambridge, a quiet little town with half our men fighting the war and most of the other half preparing to do so when they were needed. Fear was everywhere, touching everyone. It was a kind of infection that spread like the pox among all who were English, and it made men rabid in their hate. No Indian was safe to walk alone upon our streets, and even one who traveled with an English friend or master might be beaten to death. The few Indians who were not sent away to misery upon Deer Island soon vanished from our sight.

And still, no one could rest easy. A gun discharged in the middle of the night could send the whole town scampering. And so a man of our town, named Thomas Taylor, was hired to sit all night in watch. He was a doubtful fellow. His tossed hair and uncombed beard were black as a young man's, but his mouth was as sunken and toothless as a great-grandfather's.

And his clothes! You would not want to smell his clothes! But if you saw him, even from a distance, you would surely smell them. Thomas Taylor lived by doing the odd work that no one else wanted, when he wanted. Now the town hired him to stay hidden through the night at the outside of our settlement and to fire his musket if he saw savages readying for attack.

Late one night, long after I had fallen into a deep and dreamless sleep between two of my younger, squirming brothers, I woke to hear the sound of Thomas Taylor's musket. How quick I jumped up to my feet, certain that the Indians were upon us, ready to slaughter us all in our sleep. I threw open the shutter to see a general panic through the town. Men raced about in their nightshirts in the cold, raising their muskets recklessly, ready to fire. Already the drums had sounded the call to arms, and soon the church bells rang as well.

By the time I was down the stairs, my father and Sam had bolted shut the doors and taken up their muskets, waiting by open windows for the first sight of the enemy.

My mother gathered me along with the

younger children, and took us back to our rooms and closed the shutters. I did not belong among them, I told her, for was I not a printer's devil and on the way to becoming a printer? "But you must take care of the others, Bartholomew," she told me. "Make sure that they be still," she said, "as still as the dead. Otherwise King Philip will come with his Indians and send all of you quick to Heaven."

Outside, the uproar grew. I confess I was as frightened as the small children. Who could sleep on such a night, wondering if his hair would still sit upon his head in the morning?

Finally there was quiet in the streets. And I heard from below Master Gookin singing out to the night, "All is clear! Rest peaceful tonight! All is clear! Rest peaceful tonight!" No nightingale sang as sweetly.

I fell into a doze and woke to crows upon our roof calling up the sun. I did not have to be roused from bed but raced down to the kitchen.

"Some excitement, eh?" said Sam, who was still unshaved and looked as if he had not slept one moment. "Well, it was all for nothing. Old Tom Taylor had too much of Goody Gray's ale and fired off his musket only imagining an attack. Would you like to come see him?"

I followed my brother to a place near the meetinghouse that was the town jail. Out front of it, shivering with the cold, was Thomas Taylor. He stood bent over like a tree bowed down by a heavy snow, his neck and wrists set in the stocks. "Look, boy, at this disgrace of a man," Sam said loudly. And the words seemed to hurt Thomas Taylor more than the carved planks of wood that locked his arms and head into place.

"Did you and I, Sam Green, not share many a glass together?" the prisoner asked, his face twisted, his hair unruly.

"And what if we have done that? Is your shame any less?" And my brother bent over to pick up a stone from the road. And he threw it with all his might at the man in the stocks. Thomas Taylor tried to pull away, but of course could not. The rock very nearly struck his head.

By now there were others about us, although the sun was not yet fully risen from a bed of clouds that lay upon the horizon. And these others, women and children mostly, but some young men as well, began to shower miserable old Tom with clods of dirt and spoiled vegetables. Dogs were set upon him. Even I took part with the others, rubbing his hair with rotten, battered fruit. I left to finish my morning meal and begin my work in the shop. When I returned to see Tom Taylor at noon, he was alone, a loathsome, foul, and bleeding sight.

After sundown, just before his release, the constable gave him a dozen lashes by lantern light in front of the whole town. And Goody Gray herself, who had sold him his ale, rubbed salt into his wounds for good measure.

I am sorry to say that all who watched this laughed and that I was among them. I have no doubt that old Tom deserved his punishment, but it now seems wrong to make mirth at any man's misery. Freed from the stocks at last, Tom sat upon the ground weeping from his injuries, just as the saddest child cries from a nosebleed. He was lucky not to be branded on his forehead with a "D" for drunkenness. Yet he was branded in another way. Forever after, the people of Cambridge, children and adults alike, called him "False Alarm Tom," a shame that burned deeper than any branding.

Tom's false alarm did not ease our worries, but seemed to increase them. Fear ran so wild among the people that some plotted to kill all the Indians sent away to Deer Island, most of them poor, praying Indians who my father said would never have harmed us.

That spring there were English victories at last. And every one brought with it a parade of soldiers, beating their drums as they walked through the streets. These came so often that I did not always stop my work to see the marching, smiling men who carried the heads of Indian sachems mounted upon their pikes.

I was tired of war. No, I was exhausted from it, from my fingers to my brain, for every triumph meant more work for us. Still, when the news came that a feared Indian sachem named Canonchet was captured and his head taken to Hartford, even I joined the dancing around the bonfire that evening.

All the while, my Uncle Robert was growing stronger. He spent long hours with the governor, trying to persuade him that the tide of the war was with us English and that it would harm nothing to pay King Philip a ransom for the release of Annie and the other captives. Governor Leverett took pity on my uncle and finally agreed. After much pleading from my mother, my father pledged a handsome twenty pounds, but my sweet mother thought he should give even more.

"More, madam?" he said to her. "Mistress Green, have I not already done enough for your family? Let me remind you that I have paid the expenses of your brother's recovery. At this rate, I will have nothing left for my old age. I will be a pauper, just as I was when I first got off the boat from London, so poor that I had not a penny for lodging and spent my nights sleeping in a barrel."

There it was, that ancient barrel again. I worried that he would not make good on his promise to win Annie's release. "Have no fear for your old age, Father," I said, "for I will support you."

"And how shall you do that, Master Bartholomew Green? How is it you will make your living?"

"I will be a printer like you, Father," I said, "with a shop of my own."

Now my father laughed. "There's little money in that, my son. I fear we shall all be sleeping in a barrel."

For all of his complaining, my father kept his promise and paid the needed ransom. We prayed that the money would be the key that freed them all from their captivity.

One night while we were at supper in early May, there was a great rapping upon our door. I opened it to discover again that large Englishman in Indian leather, the trapper John Hoar. He followed me into the kitchen where he and my father greeted one another, each in his turn shaking the other by the shoulders with teeth-rattling vigor.

"Is there news of the captives?" my father asked.

"Yes, there is news," Master Hoar said. "For I have delivered the ransom myself to King Philip and his followers. There are some who say I trade in captives, that I'm in the business of trading human souls," he said.

"I have not heard that said about you," my father said.

"It *is* said about me. I know this," said Master Hoar. "Some people compare me to a slave trader. Well, you know, Samuel, I have no use for slave traders. No use for them at all. I make no profit in arranging ransoms for the release of captives. Not a cent have I made. The good will of men is all I seek."

"And you have mine," my father said. "But what news have you, John?"

"Oh, I have more than news," the trapper said. "I have the captives themselves, and by this time, they should be outside your door."

My father and I rushed to the door and flung it open. My Uncle Robert and the others were close behind us. There, standing in front of our house, were three horses, their breath like smoke in the cool, damp night.

Holding their reins were two men dressed in leather with fur-skin caps upon their heads. They were Indians. But they did not carry either knives or muskets, and their faces were not painted.

Still sitting upon the horses were three haggard women, dressed in ragged dresses.

At first, I must admit, I recognized none of them. I looked at one of them, a girl with dark eyes and sunken cheeks. She was so thin that a breath of wind might have blown her from her horse's back. I was not sure I knew her.

"Why do you stare at me so, Bartholomew?" Annie said. "Have I changed so?"

Yes, she had changed, grown taller like a reed, but frail at the same time, like an old, sickly woman. Yet I did not say so. "I hoped it was you, Annie," I said.

She jumped down and grabbed me by my neck and pulled me toward her. "How can you not know me?" she cried. "Have I been gone so long that I am forgotten?"

"I could never forget you," I said.

Next she went to my uncle. "Oh, Father," Annie said. "I thought I might never see you again."

"Nor I you, when last I saw you. Never in this world," Uncle Robert said.

One of the women still on horseback began to cough and cry and carry on. And right away, I knew that this was my aunt, who looked very poorly. My Uncle Robert helped her down and to her feet. She was so slight a person that she seemed to disappear in his arms.

I did not recognize the third rider, even after

much staring. Master Hoar helped her dismount. She was uneasy on her feet.

"This, good friends, is Mistress Mary White Rowlandson, who asks if she may stay the night," said Master Hoar.

"Of course," my mother said. "You shall stay as long as you like."

"I know of this family, even if you do not know me," Mistress Rowlandson said. "The books you have printed were on the shelves of our house at Lancaster." Her voice was loud and sure, far stronger than her sad appearance.

My father bid them all join us at supper, the two Indian men included, for they, too, were tired and hungry from their journey. Inside, with food and warmth, the captives began to melt a little, to come again to life. All but my poor aunt, who was overcome with fits of coughing. My mother took her off to bed, treating her with tenderness as if she were a sick child.

The rest of us talked for a while. The hour grew late, but what work was still to be done that night in the printing shop could wait.

At first, it was Mary Rowlandson who did much of the talking in a lively voice in spite of her weariness. There was a madness about her appearance as she sat by the fire, with her gown torn and her fine hair, which was the color of straw, all in tangles.

"Master Green, were it not for your apprentice, we would have died in King Philip's camp," she said. "I was taken at Lancaster on the tenth of February, my beloved daughter dying in my arms. When I came to King Philip's camp after a journey of almost three weeks, I was near dead from my wounds.

"Of all the Indians in that camp, only James was of comfort to me. He bid me to be of good cheer and said that he would speak to King Philip about my release. And this he did along with other good deeds. He gave me tobacco, which I was able to exchange for food. He gave me bits of cloth, which I did sew into English aprons, which were greatly valued by the Indian women.

"When I would not eat, he told me that I must, even if the soup was made of horses' hooves and the smell most foul.

"He brought Annie to me, to nurse me when I was still sick. And he told Master John Hoar that for a jug of liquor, my master in King Philip's camp, the wicked sachem Quanopin, would agree to release me.

"It was King Philip himself who set my ransom at twenty pounds, and James who wrote the ransom note just as Philip told him. Good Master Green, if your apprentice requires a good word to win his pardon when this war is done, I am one who would gladly give it."

"Still it shames me that he has gone to the enemy's camp," my father said.

"Have no shame for him, Uncle Samuel," Annie said. She had been sitting quietly by herself. "Without him, I, too, would be lost. After we were captured, we were five days on the journey to King Philip's camp. We had to run to keep up with the others, for if we fell behind we were prodded with sticks and severely beaten.

"James watched over us to stop the beatings when he could and to see that we had enough food and water.

"When we came to King Philip's camp, James sent my mother and me to the wickiup of his friend Sagamore Tom, who was once a praying Indian. We were treated kindly by him, no different from the way he treated his own children. At the end of the day, he liked me to read to him from the Bible and I did so with great happiness. But I wondered if he prayed for a victory over the English just as I prayed that his people be defeated.

"One day, James took me to King Philip, who remembered me from the day we saw him in Boston, Bartholomew. He told me that I had grown and was not a child anymore but a woman, and would fetch a good price from the English.

"James told me, 'Be of good cheer, Annie. It will not be so long before you are ransomed and released.' So you see, Uncle, I have no kinder, dearer friend in all the world than James."

The next morning, my father declared that there would be no work in the printing shop. Sam and I caught two geese and five large hens. And we did slaughter and help to pluck them. Goody Gray, hobbling now with aching joints, came with buckets of ale and cider and breads and cakes. "We shall have a feast!" my father said as he counted out the coins for Goody Gray.

All the while, my mother helped Annie and the others with warm baths and found clothes for them.

By noon the whole town had heard news of the captives' release. And the church bells rang, and all our neighbors came by, and many stayed with us for a day of feasting. I know that some say today that the Puritans of my youth were a sad and brooding lot. But if only they could have seen us on this day of rejoicing, for our grins were large and our hearts full to bursting.

And yet the captives themselves were not as glad as those who received them. My aunt stayed in bed, too sick to raise her head. And my cousin spent much time beside her. Only Mary Rowlandson seemed merry. Yet even she acted strangely. Often I saw her seated away from the others, never letting go of her Bible, whispering its soothing words to herself. In the early evening, my father sent me to the brewer's shop for more ale, and Annie asked if she might come with me.

As we walked in the darkness, the moon not

yet high, she held me tightly. And when an owl sounded, she gripped my arm so fiercely that I was sure I would see marks upon it in the morning.

"What frightens you?" I asked her.

"Everything frightens me," she said. "I have seen things too horrible to tell. And with every bird cry or horse's whinny, I hear an Indian giving signal to a new attack."

We walked in silence all the rest of the way.

In the morning, Sam helped Mistress Rowlandson upon our wagon and took her in to Boston, to be reunited with her husband.

In the next days, as the flowers began to open in the joy of spring, Annie's mother grew ever more gravely ill, despite my mother's careful nursing. Even bleeding did nothing to restore her strength, but seemed to make her weaker. All day she coughed and gasped for breath. At night she thrashed about so violently that she could not be left alone. After many days of this, she seemed to tire of her struggle to stay on this earth.

My mother opened her shutters by day and filled her room with candles at night so that there was always light about her. She was never alone. My uncle stayed by her and Annie did, too, and they tried to help her rest when she was racked with coughing.

But she grew no better. And one night, she grew suddenly very quiet, shuddered, and slipped away. Many died in Cambridge during that winter and spring, of flux or croup or other disease, more than died at the hands of the savages. There was no one to accuse, but people still did blame the Indians, as they did for all their sorrows.

Annie and her father stayed on with us for a time, the two of them slowly regaining health, if not happiness. I did what I could to cheer my cousin, but my own days were spent in the printing shop, for there was much work to be done. Every victory meant another proclamation to be posted. So did every Indian raid and massacre. And who should print them, but Samuel Green and his sons?

Our house was so filled with visitors that I slept upon a pallet in the printing shop. Annie was no longer strong enough for the heavy labor there, but every night she came by with my father after supper to sort type. And Goody Gray would come by to bring us news of the war. It was as it had been before the war. But it was also very different.

"Where is James this night?" I wondered aloud.

"Hiding and skulking," said Goody Gray, rocking back and forth while drinking too much of her own ale.

"No, Goody," Annie said. "He is a kind and decent man."

"No kind and decent man would be party to King Philip and his savages."

"But if he was not there, I would have been killed, and so would my dear father."

"That's true," said Goody Gray. "It is providence that put him there, my dear girl, so that you could find your way home again."

My father was turning the pages of his account books. "I suppose it was providence that put me here so that I might spend a great many pounds to win the girl's release, eh, Goody Gray?" he said.

"So it was," the old woman said. "So it was."

Yet for all his spending to release my cousin and her mother, the war was good for my father's account books, with all the printing to be done. In June, Governor Leverett sent to us a special notice to be broadly circulated by Master Hoar and Master Gookin and many others who traveled among the Indians. The notice was short, and I said I could set it myself.

"What a printer's devil I have in you!" my father said. "I have never seen the like of it in someone of your tender years. You'll be apprenticed before you know it! Why, James will come back and find his job is taken!"

The proclamation said that in fourteen days, all Indians at large in Massachusetts Bay should surrender themselves to Governor Leverett. Those who did so would be forgiven their misdeeds during the war. But those who did not would be punished when the war was over.

My father held up the proof sheet and admired it. "Let us hope," he said, "that these words will be as good as bullets and put an end to the fighting."

The proclamation proved that there was magic in words. Soon Indians were coming into towns like ours to lay down their arms and give themselves up. One of the first who came into Cambridge was an old chief, or sachem, known as Captain William, who rode in upon a horse and gave himself up to Master Gookin.

Captain William was a praying Indian, a chief of the Nipmuck. And before the rebellion, he was an assistant to our friend and neighbor, Master Gookin. Together they held court to judge the misdeeds of Indians by the standards of English law. At first during the war, he stayed loyal to the English, but he refused to be taken to Deer Island with the others. Instead, he ran away to join the rebels.

How William was treated would show how the English could be merciful in victory. My father knew Captain William, and Master Gookin asked that he journey to Boston to speak for him. He drove our wagon so that Annie and I could go with him. "I want you to see," he said, "how we English can be as generous in victory as we were fierce in battle."

We sat upon the seat next to him. Master Gookin and Captain William sat behind us in the bed of the wagon. The way was slow, but it was a fine day and my father and Master Gookin talked happily. They said it was certain that there would be peace before summer.

Captain William was a large man. And his face was made fierce by black marks upon his nose and mouth that would not wash off no matter how strong the soap or stiff the brush. If these were the markings of war, then Captain William's face could be said to be always ready for battle. To soften his looks, Master Gookin had seen to it that his hair was cut in the English way. He was also given an English coat and hat to wear. But no jacket could be found large enough for his enormous body or cap big enough for his huge head. So he looked as if he were wearing another man's clothing, perhaps stolen from a fallen Englishman.

We drove to the house of Governor Leverett, who was expecting our arrival. Outside there was a restless crowd, which stopped our wagon a hundred feet from the governor's door. There was Lemuel Brown again, exciting the crowd, lifting his eye patch and blaming Captain William for the loss of his long-lost eye. The mob soon began throwing rocks and vegetables at the poor Indian. Master Gookin jumped to his feet in a fury. "Is this the way we English keep our promises? Be ashamed if we cannot keep our word, for we are worse than the savages." He pushed through the crowd, shouting as he moved with Captain William at his side, and we followed. I held tight to

Annie's hand until we were safely inside the governor's house, the door safely closed and bolted.

Governor Leverett came down to meet us. He wore clothing of black cloth, and his face was surrounded by a white, wimpled collar. He seemed startled to see the giant Indian with the painted face.

"Good heavens, Master Gookin," he said, "you bring him without shackles?"

"There was no need, your honor," Master Gookin said. "He comes willingly to claim his pardon."

My father said, "He has been of no trouble to us, your excellency. We know him to be a gentle man."

The governor looked Captain William over as if he were studying the poor fit of his clothes.

"Was this man an ordinary soldier or was he one of their chiefs?" he asked.

"He is a chief among the Nipmuck, Master Leverett," said Master Gookin. "And before these wars he was an assistant to me, a kind of clerk when I was judge of English law among the Indians."

"He is one of their sagamores, then," said the

governor, walking around Captain William as he spoke. "These were the mischief makers. Them we hold responsible. Not like the ordinary Indian who did what he was told."

Captain William spoke up for the first time. "I beg for your pardon, your excellency." And the large man dropped to his knees and bowed his head.

Governor Leverett whispered something to a servant. While Captain William still kneeled, the servant came back with two soldiers, one holding chains and the other armed with a gun that he aimed at the Indian's heart.

"Rise up, Captain William," the governor said. When the Indian obeyed the command, the chains were locked about his ankles. They hung loosely enough so that he could walk but not run. That done, Governor Leverett bid his soldiers, "Take this fellow to the jailhouse and commend him to Captain James Oliver's keeping."

Without thinking, Annie shouted out, "You cannot do that! He has come for the pardon you yourself offered to all! You must set him free!"

I knew she was right about what the governor promised, because I had set the type myself. Frail as she still was, Annie should have been severely punished for speaking so to his excellency, the governor of Massachusetts Bay, Master John Leverett. Or to any other adult. But Master Gookin stepped forward to take her part. "Sir, you cannot do this! He has surrendered on the promise of a pardon, and pardoned he must be."

Governor John Leverett was angry now. "Master Gookin, sir, how dare you interfere! I am the elected governor and do not act on my own behalf but for the safety of the people I serve. The ordinary Indian, whether or not he was a soldier against us, will be taken to Deer Island until the war is done. But the sagamores, the chiefs in this rebellion, they must answer to the General Court. The one called Captain William will have a chance to make his case before a magistrate tomorrow. If he was not one of the mischief makers, he has nothing to fear. But if he was one of them, leading others to burn towns and kill English men and women, then he must pay for these offenses."

Now my father spoke. "But, your honor, the council did not say this in its proclamation. I know the words well. This son of mine set them in type, and I printed them myself."

The governor was in a fury, his face red with rage. "How many of these villains will come to us freely, if they know they must answer for their foul offenses?"

"Then it is a dishonest trick," said Master Gookin, now swinging his hands wildly as he spoke. "And it will soon work against your intent. For who will come forward of his own accord if he knows he will be punished?"

"Master Gookin, sir, and you, my friend, Master Green," Governor Leverett began. His anger had vanished like a puff of smoke before the wind. "Please do not be unreasonable. If your friend is as you say, he will be fairly treated. We are English gentlemen and wish no harm to any but those who merit it."

And so, poor Captain William was taken away by the two soldiers. We watched as the three of them moved through the crowd. The Indian looked back upon us and shouted, "Pray for me, sirs. For I have never harmed the English. Before God, I am innocent." And I remembered the Indian called Little John, who said those same few words just before he was hoisted up by his neck upon the Boston Common.

Master Gookin stayed on in Boston, but my father sadly took my cousin and me home. "We have seen enough senseless slaughter," he said.

Captain William was hanged the next day.

But not all Indian sachems were treated in so terrible a fashion. The squaw sachem Awashonks promised to fight against King Philip and all Indians who stood by him. She and her warriors were to be spared all punishment for their many misdeeds. The end of the war was near. The night of her surrender, we had yet another bonfire upon the commons, and I saw that wars end as they begin, with great fires and celebration. And I frolicked with the rest. But Annie sat by her father through the night and prayed.

CHAPTER NINE

RETURN

THE WAR DID NOT END IN A SINGLE MOMENT; rather, each new day brought little victories. More and more rebel Indians came home to claim their pardons. Whole tribes came over to the English side.

Near the end of June, with the summer's heat full upon us, Governor Leverett declared a day of thanksgiving, and my brother Sam left me to set the type. Alone, I finished the job by candlelight. When the work was done and the last candle snuffed, I lay down upon my pallet by the printing press and fell at once to sleep.

Nothing, I thought, could wake me. If a fire ran through the print shop, it would have consumed me, so weary was I. And yet, a man's voice disturbed my sleep. It was soft and breathless. "Bartholomew!" it said with urgency. "Bartholomew, you must wake up and do me service." The words sent chills through me, as if they had been spoken by a dead man. I started to shout out his name, but his hand covered my mouth.

When he removed his hand, I spoke to him softly. "I knew you would come, James," I said. "How glad I am that you are still alive."

"I am glad of it, too," he said. "Just two days ago, an old English woman fired upon me from the window of her house, and I could hear the lead fly by my ear. And this morning I was almost shot by an old sagamore who wanted my horse. If he had not recognized me at the last, I would certainly be dead.

"This was my friend, Sagamore Tom, into whose care I trusted Annie and her mother.

And he did treat them like his own children. I felt such pity for him that I gave him the horse."

"How did you come to own a horse?" I asked.

"King Philip himself gave it to me when we parted. He made a joke of it, saying if the animal were not so thin, we would have eaten him long ago."

"Did you bring King Philip with you?" I asked, frightened now.

"No, Bartholomew. All the sagamores have scattered to the winds. When last I saw King Philip, he was heading home upon a better horse than mine."

"Will he ask to be pardoned?"

"He knows there can be no pardon for him, even if he begs for one. No more than there was for poor Captain William."

"What of you, James? Will you be pardoned?"

"I will need your help to remain among the living," he said.

He had me light a lamp for him and then he wrote out a note, while I studied his appearance. James looked different now. Perhaps it

190

was the dancing flame, but he seemed thin, even gaunt. His cheeks were sunken, and his eyes seemed older and more weary. Even in an English hat and coat, he looked more Indian than I remembered, his skin weathered and dark.

"Take this note to your father and Master Gookin," he commanded me. "Show it to no others! My life depends upon it!"

I ran across the meadow and down the street to my family's house. I was able to rouse my father from his slumber without waking up my mother. He dressed hastily, adding a scarf and his red cap to protect his hairless head, even though the night was warm and balmy. The two of us were soon knocking upon Master Gookin's door most loudly, until he admitted us. With Master Gookin in the lead, we were not long arriving at the printer's shop, where James sat silently in the dark.

Gookin was the first to speak as I lighted a lamp. "I was not sure these blurry old eyes would ever see your face again," he said. "You are as welcome here as a returning son. Soon we will have you working at the press as before."

My father was equally happy. "Master Eliot still talks of a new Indian Bible. One without the mistakes of the old one, that the savages will not laugh at, and he says you are the one to help him with his translation. And you know what that means to an honest printer. Three years' work at a good wage paid in English coin. And you shall be entitled to your share, an apprentice no longer."

James smiled now. "I wish it to be so," he said.

"And why not?" my father said. "The governor will give you the pardon he has promised. Master Eliot will insist! *I* will insist upon it!"

"Just as he promised Captain William," James said without anger, but sadly. "I do not want to end my days hanging from a rope. If that is my fate, it would be better to be killed by an English musket."

"Trust in God," said Master Gookin.

"And did not Captain William trust in God? It is Governor Leverett I do not trust."

"You are right, there," Gookin said. "We cannot allow the governor and the General Court to repeat that terrible mistake. You must stay here, away from sight, while I talk to the governor and set the terms of your surrender."

For two whole days, James hid away in an empty room above the printing shop. He was to stay quiet all the day, while my brother Sam and I printed three hundred copies of the governor's thanksgiving declaration, to be taken to the farthest reaches of our colony. But all the while we worked, we waited for the news from Master Gookin.

Late on that second afternoon, Master Gookin returned with my father to the printing shop. Annie, dressed in dark clothes and looking a grown-up woman, came with them. I took all three to James's room, being careful not to be noticed by the college students.

James was too restless to be seated.

"Captain Moseley spoke against you, as you might have expected," Master Gookin said. "He called you demon and deceiver, and said your conduct during the war was proof that you were no praying Indian but a lying heathen. It was awful how he carried on against you. But there were others there.

"Mistress Rowlandson and her husband, the

good pastor, spoke in your defense. And when that gentlewoman spoke, it brought a quiet to all who came to talk against you. Even Lemuel Brown held his spiteful tongue after her account of your good deeds, for how could *he* deny them?

"And then, to drive the nail home, Mistress Annie Clark here rose to speak in your behalf. When she described how you had saved her and her father from certain scalping, the case was settled in your favor! Now the score is even, for you owe this young woman your life as she owes you hers."

Annie said to James, "Oh, I was not alone. Many in the room cried out in your behalf."

"Then I am pardoned?" James asked.

Annie and Master Gookin now fell silent, leaving it to my father to say the rest.

"Yes," he said, "you are pardoned. But with conditions."

"Conditions?" James asked. "What conditions?"

"These great and sober men who rule us worry about the opinion of the general rabble," my father said. "They worry that your kindness to the captives will be seen as but a sham to win your pardon. And so they ask for proof of your faithfulness to the laws of the English."

"I will give them whatever proof they ask of me," James said. "Tell me what it is I must do."

Annie, who had been sitting down, now rose up and ran from the room, crying, "It is too terrible for me to listen!"

Master Gookin walked up to James and put his hands upon his shoulders. I could see that he was in tears as he spoke. "Governor Leverett says that the General Court has agreed to forgive any and all of your misdeeds. But as a sign of your regard for English authority, you must bring them two heads."

"Heads?" James laughed. "Of wolves, or bears, or cows? For two heads I will bring them, if that is their only price."

Master Gookin shook his head. "Two heads of Indians," he said.

James sputtered his reply. "Two heads from me, who never has raised his hand in anger against Indian or English?"

"That is what the governor asks of you, my friend," Master Gookin said.

"Then I am doomed," James said. And now he wept as a child would, and I was glad that Annie was not there to see it.

That night, my father saw that James had a good supper and gave him a knife that was sharpened well. By the time I awoke the next morning, James was gone.

A week went by, and the business of the shop went on. But my heart was not in my work. I thought constantly of James. Where could he run to find a place outside the English law?

I was asleep by the press one night when I was awakened by the cry of an owl in its flight. The door to the printing shop opened and James walked in, carrying a round deerskin bag. I said nothing, acting as if I did not hear him enter. He curled up on the floor and went to sleep.

Next morning, I wanted to ask about the bag, but he stopped me, saying that I should fetch my father and Master Gookin. At my father's command, Sam drove our wagon by the printing shop and James slipped into the back, where he lay hidden under a cloth cover. My brother, my father, Master Gookin, and I took him straight away to Boston on that early summery afternoon, the second of July, 1676. Annie wanted to go, but her father would not allow it.

With James still in the wagon, my father knocked upon Governor Leverett's door. A servant let him in, and, after many minutes, my father came for the rest of us.

Governor Leverett stood before us without his coat on. While he stood, none of us could sit. Although it was a hot day, he offered us nothing to satisfy our thirst. We could say nothing until he did, and he was in no hurry.

Finally, he spoke directly to James. "You have been the cause of great mischief among us English. In another case, we would have seen you hanged upon the gallows here. But your friends say that you are a good and Christian man. For that reason, we agreed to pardon you, but only if you give us signs of your loyalty and good intent. Have you brought us the signs we asked for?"

James's face, usually so full of spirit, was blank as any piece of paper. Usually so talkative, he said nothing, but reached into his bag. One by one, he pulled out the remains of what had once been human heads, holding them by their long, black hair. He held them high above us, not just to show us but to horrify.

"These I have cut from the corpses of my fallen comrades," he said. "I have done as you have asked."

This brave governor, who had seen much combat, now gasped at the sight and the smell of these terrible trophies. For a while, I wondered if I would breathe again or would be struck down in fright.

My father stepped in front of me so that I might not see any longer and said, "It's enough. Put them away. This is too much for the boy." And James did as my father told him.

"Now you will release him?" my father asked Governor Leverett.

Master Leverett seemed surprised. "I cannot release him. He would not be safe upon the streets of either Boston or Cambridge, or any-place where English men and women dwell. For his sake, I must keep him." And the governor ordered that James be taken at once to the jailhouse to wait for his passage to Deer Island.

James looked at me and cried out, "I am lost." He was shackled and taken away.

But the governor kept his word. There was no general announcement of James's imprisonment. No crowd gathered outside the jail to demand that he be taken to the gallows. Early the next morning, before Lemuel Brown or any of the others of his kind could learn of James's capture, he was put into a small boat and rowed to Deer Island, where his father and two of his brothers still dwelled.

As for the heads, Governor Leverett ordered that they be placed upon long poles and set upon the commons alongside the heads of Little John and Captain William and the many others. These most gruesome decorations were to be a warning to anyone who might dare rise against the English. But in time, nothing remained of them but barest skulls, bleached white by the weather, grinning at those who stared upon them. They were so changed by time that they might have been English skulls instead of Indian. And they took on a different meaning from the one intended, for they spoke of the cruelty of the English against their vanquished foe.

A few days later, my father and I rowed out to Deer Island to visit James under a soldier's watchful eye. We came with sacks of cornmeal and pickled meats and the fruits of our garden. What we saw there was as terrible as any battle scene. Disease had done the work of warfare. Only a few of these Indians slept in regular wigwams, sealed tight against the fog and foul weather that blew in across the bay. The rest slept under little sheds that provided little protection. We found James with his father, old Priambow. They said that they lived on clams and fish and what roots and nuts they could find upon this barren island.

But many of the others had lost heart or were sick, and had become skeletons even as they lived. Even the youngest seemed old and weary of living.

I said good-bye to James, unsure I would ever see him again. "Remember me, Bartholomew," he said as we departed the island. And how could I not remember him?

A few days later, Sagamore Tom was captured and put to death because the horse he rode was believed to belong to a man killed in the Hatfield massacre. He told the court that the horse was a gift. But the animal was easily recognized, for the owner had cut three notches in the horse's right ear.

And one by one, the sachems were put to death or died fleeing from the victorious English. Soon King Philip himself was found, sitting peacefully upon a log not far from his home. He was captured easily. He did not put up a fight. But he was shot through the heart by an Indian named Alderman, who wanted to show his devotion to the English. His body was cut into four pieces and left in the trees for crows. For his pains, Alderman was given King Philip's hand, which he carried with him for the rest of his life. An odd reward, I thought, for one man's treachery to his brother.

King Philip's head was taken to the governor of Plymouth, who placed it upon a pole for all to see. I know that it remains there still, for I saw it myself, a slack-jawed skull gazing out on the people of Plymouth and haunting their dreams. Gone were the gleaming dark eyes I remembered that could grapple with a man's soul. But even the bare bones of that large skull were frightening to behold, with its shadowy caves and long-toothed smile.

As for James, he and his family stayed on Deer Island until the following spring. They were among the few who survived that terrible winter of imprisonment. When the time came for their release, none was allowed to stay in Boston or Cambridge, not the kindest of workmen or the most devoted slave. Many returned to the praying villages, to Natick or Hassenamesitt, where they lived more or less like Englishmen, but separate. Others traveled farther away, to the French lands to the north or west over the mountains, beyond the reach of all but a few settlers and traders.

I did not see James in those first years. But I heard that he worked at his crops at Hassenamesitt until his hands grew coarse from the labor. He did marry a woman said to be half-Indian and half-English, and they had children, all called by the name of Printer, as if James had been born to it.

As for me, of course, I became an apprentice in my father's shop, a printer's devil no longer! My brother Sam, ever restless, left for Hartford to start his own press there. Halfway through my apprenticeship, Master Eliot, ancient and gnarled as an old apple tree, came into our shop with a commission for his new Indian Bible. He said that James would return to work with us, for we would need every hand that we could find now that Sam was away. Permission would be granted for him to live as he had done before, in the print shop of the Indian school at Harvard.

James, who once had been so full of talk, spoke little now as he worked. Yet often he would complain to me if a line of type was not perfectly straight or if I had dropped a needed letter from a word or inserted an unneeded one. "This book," he said, "will be remembered long after you and I have left this earth, and we must make it right."

I could see that he had changed. He was far too somber now. All the play had left him. And when at first I asked him about the war and especially about that great villain King Philip, with his war paint of red and blue, James would only say, "Those days are best forgotten. Do not speak of them."

How very old Master Eliot seemed when he came around with the latest revisions to the manuscript. He walked with a limp now, as if every bone of his body ached with every step.

His hands shook so that the papers shivered in his fingers as he handed them to James. But he did not complain, and his eyes were as bright and fearless as they had ever been.

James treated him with wonderful courtesy. It was in the spring in the year of 1679 when the work began. And James found again the rhythm of his work, as if he had never lost it, the click-click-click of lead letters slapped into place, for hours at a time. To my shame, he was still far faster than I.

Often we worked at the press, standing side by side, pulling around the lever that would imprint the Indian words onto paper. And when I complained that I could not read this text, written in his strange tongue and full of double "k's" and many "q's," he said, "A printer does not need to understand. The letters are what matter."

Yet, every printer I have ever known cares about the meaning of these ink spots upon a page. And I do believe that James did care, for when a word was wrong he would rip up the proof sheet and reset whole pages at a time. For it can be said that no one understood the strength, the magic, of words as much as he.

My father still bustled about the shop, but he left most of the work to James and me. He was forever calculating and recalculating his payments and expenses. But when the proof sheets were struck, no one had a better eye for a broken letter or a crooked line.

We worked at it six full days each week. In a little over a year, we had finished with the New Testament and bound some five hundred of these into a pretty little volume. Next we began setting the Old Testament, an even longer work that would take us years. We began each day before first light and scarcely stopped until long after the sun had set. By the end of each day my fingers ached to the touch of lead and fine paper. Other laborers might grow sick and be forced to stop their work, but we dared not.

"I must see this work done before I die," Master Eliot would say, if one of us grew sick for a time or begged for rest.

Yet sometimes, when Master Eliot was not to be seen, my father would take in other, much smaller, jobs as well.

Much to our surprise, into our shop one day came Mistress Mary Rowlandson. She greeted my father and me warmly. But she treated

James as if he were the governor or the king himself, taking his hand and curtsying before him. She was not so bone white now as when I saw her last, and her cheeks were flushed and healthy as if she had dabbed them with a rosy color, as some women do these days.

"Master Printer," she said to James, "I have a manuscript for you." She handed him a sheaf of papers. "It is the tale of my captivity. The bookseller, Master Usher, wants one thousand copies of this little book. He wanted it printed on the new press in Boston, but I said it was more fitting that your hand should set my words in type."

"That will not be possible, Mistress Rowlandson," my father said. "For all his time is promised to Master Eliot's Bible. But my son, Bartholomew, could turn his hand to this and do it as well as if I set the type myself."

"That will not do," Mistress Rowlandson said. "For I promised myself when I was freed from King Philip's camp that I would not forget James's kindness. This little book is his reward, and yours, too, Master Green, for you will find much profit in it."

The word "profit" never failed to bring my father to life, no matter how tired or occupied. It ignited him the way a match does light a fire.

He bowed to Mistress Rowlandson. "I think that our James can make quick work of this," he said. So it was that James set all the type. And he proofed each page himself so that he might read it. He was moved almost to tears, not just by the words themselves and the account of her suffering, but by memories of friends that the words revived. Philip was there. And Sagamore Tom. And Master Hoar. And to his own surprise, he found himself in the type that he set by his own hand, click-click-click. She wrote that her Indian master Quanopin, "went out of the wigwam and by and by sent in an Indian called James the Printer, who told Mr. Hoar that my master would let me go home tomorrow if he would let him have one pint of liquors."

James knew that was not everything. She told only the smallest part of the story and often left out the most important part. But still, there was James, a name whispered in black marks upon a page, to be heard one day by his own children and their children's children, long after he had left the earth.

When the printing of her book was done, we folded the pages together using sticks of antler bone. Then James, my father, and I bound them up between leather covers and shipped them off to Master Usher's shop. Never did a book sell so many copies so quickly. And it was not long before James and I had to set the type again for another edition. And another. All over New England, men knew the name of Mary Rowlandson and cried over her suffering as if it were fresh.

All the while, the work on Master Eliot's Indian Bible continued. Soon every storage bin was filled and all the tables. Finished sheets were stacked upon each other, squared off in rectangular blocks like houses, a little village of them rising up inside our printing shop.

"I will die before it's done, I know it," Master Eliot often said.

"It will be the death of me," said my father.

In 1685, fully six years after the work had begun, James and I began sewing whole books together, binding them in the best quality deerskin. How pleased we were when it was done.

And it did not matter to us that neither of our names appeared upon the title page. "Printed by Samuel Green," it said, in two different languages, English and Algonquian. But we knew the work was ours.

The next morning, my father handed that first finished copy to Master Eliot. He held it in his shaking hands as tenderly as a newborn child. He turned it over, examining every inch of the deer hide. Then he opened it and turned the pages, running his long fingers over the black letters as if he could feel the imprint upon the page and read it with a touch.

He said to James, "You remember the day when I first read to you from a book like this?"

"I cannot forget it," James said. "It was the first day of my life."

Now Master Eliot handed the book to James. "This book is properly yours, not mine. I am happy enough to live to see this day. This book, it is a little miracle."

James took the book, and he, too, turned it in his hands. "I, too, never thought that I would live to see this," he said.

Many months later, when all the books were bound, James moved away. My father gave him twenty pounds owed him at the end of his apprenticeship. And that allowed him to purchase some land for a house near Hassenamesitt, near the English town of Grafton.

I ended my apprenticeship just two years later. With the fifty pounds my father gave me, I moved to Boston, where the main printing work of all New England was being done. There were many printers in Boston and many presses and much competition among them. My brother Sam returned to Boston about this time, and he and my father and I sometimes were given work to do together. But then Sam died of the pox, and I spent much time at work with my grieving father.

The years flew by like the flocks of geese winging their way to the south every fall, quickly and with great majesty. I married, and my sweet wife, Mary, bore ten children, all but two of them now grown to adulthood. My cousin Annie married also, to a merchant who owned more than a dozen ships that brought thousands more Englishmen here to New England. I became the printer of a newspaper, the *Boston News-letter*. Many years later I was able to purchase it. Like my father before me, I became the printer of the laws of Massachusetts Bay, a handsome position that assured a profit and my prosperity.

Sometimes we heard of James Printer. Little things. There was a property dispute with some English near Grafton, which he and his cousin John Wampus were able to settle by trading some of their lands. He was a man of considerable property. And I heard that he devoted much time among the Indians, teaching them to read in English and in their native Algonquian.

I saw him once, at the funeral of Master John Eliot. More than a thousand people came to it, to pin a note of remembrance upon the old man's coffin as was the custom. Annie pointed James out to me. He stood beside Master Eliot's coffin, dressed like a prosperous merchant, wearing white gloves and a high hat. I could not shout out to him, but Annie and I pressed through the crowd to try to catch hold of him. But when I reached the spot where I had seen James, who should be standing there but Lemuel Brown, the same one who had accused Little John and Captain William. "How dare the likes of him, that printer, show up at a solemn occasion such as this," Brown was telling the crowd. "Some of us will not forget how he betrayed us during the war, sneaking away to be with that villain, King Philip himself. So I says to him, this printer James, I says, 'Even I who has but one eye can see you. How dare you show your face among good English folk like us.' And I would have beat him with my walking stick if he did not disappear in this crowd before I could land a single blow upon him."

But for the memory of good John Eliot I would have set upon this Lemuel Brown with *my* walking stick. Instead, I said, "That printer has more right to be here than you do, Lemuel Brown. Be gone with you before I have the sheriff send you on your way!"

And this maker of trouble between people did run away from me, because he knew I knew him.

It was many years later before I saw James again. In 1709, my wife died. My cousin Annie, by then a widow, kindly agreed to help run my household. As glum as I was, Annie tried all the harder to keep me of good cheer.

One day at dinner, a Master Experience Mayhew came to call. He had translated a psalm book into the Indian tongue and asked me to print it for him. He thought it would be useful for his preaching among the Indians.

"You alone among printers today have experience in printing in Algonquian," he said.

I laughed out loud at his words. "Oh, you are very wrong there, Master Mayhew," I said. "There is one printer who has more ability than I, one who reads and writes in Algonquian. He is the right printer for your job."

So it was that I rode out one fine fall morning in search of James Printer. At the end of a long day, I came to the town of Grafton, where I stayed at a little inn. The keepers there knew of James and directed me to his house. The next morning, I found it, not far off a large road, a fine, three-storied house with many gables.

And there inside was my old friend and teacher.

When I reached for his hand, he grabbed hold of me and pulled me to him. "I have heard much of your success, Bartholomew," he said.

We talked awhile of old times, but then I told him my purpose. "I have a commission for you," I said. "A job of printing in the Indian tongue and in English."

He seemed surprised. "It is so long since I have been a printer," he said. "I am now a printer in name only."

"Your skills have not faded," I said.

"Oh, they have all but disappeared," he said.

"You'll remember them quickly," I said. "No one else but you can do this job. It is to be a book in two languages, English and Algonquian, side by side on each page. And who but you can set and read the Algonquian? It is but a little job. Won't you consent?"

"Only if we stand together side by side while the work is done," James said.

"And we will race against each other?" I asked.

"Of course," he said. "We must see if the pupil has at last surpassed the master."

So it was that James came to stay with me in Boston, and we worked on one last book. For weeks, James and I and Annie had all of our meals together and talked as we did of old. What anger there was in him after the war

214

seemed to have left him. And he laughed now at the memory of the wounds I suffered when my brother Sam threw type at me.

Every day, we worked together at my shop, racing as we did years ago to see who could finish his column of type before the other. Soon, it was clear that he was as fast as I. And through this competition, we finished the book in a few weeks time.

Late one night, I wandered back into the shop alone to set the final page. By lantern light I did sew together the signatures of the first of the books in a jacket of vellum.

The next morning, Annie was there when I handed him this finished book, holding it open so he could see the title page.

He smiled at what I had done, just as he smiled often upon me when I was a boy in those days before King Philip's War began. For this is what I had printed, first in Algonquian: "Upprinthomunneau B. Green, kah J. Printer." And then in English: "Printed by B. Green and J. Printer."

"So at last," James said, now laughing with pleasure, "I am a real printer. For now these words do tell me so."

Annie and I, too, began laughing at the joke that only the three of us could understand.

Laughter has a way of using itself up. And when we had finished with it, tears ran from my eyes, for I knew I had righted a great wrong against him. I took hold of James's hands and said, "Truly there is no greater printer in all New England. And now, all the world will be able to read it, in English and Indian alike."

He tried to speak, but had trouble doing so. Suddenly, he looked like the old man he was, almost three score and ten, at the end of his allotted days. Yes, he was crying, but with pleasure, reading over and over those words in English and Indian, his name and mine on the same title page.

"Look," he said, "look at the magic that words can make. They bring us together for all men to see, Indians and English, now and ever after." I nodded my agreement.

"Oh, the magic," he said. "The magic of words, of black marks upon white paper!"

Afterword

I WAS SITTING IN THE RARE BOOKS COLLECTION at Harvard University, just a few steps from where James Printer once lived and worked. A librarian handed me the book I had asked for—presenting it to me in a box, as if it were a present. Inside was an old volume bound in deerskin, marred only a little by the centuries, with stains of ordinary handling and small holes left behind by long-dead insects. I turned the volume over carefully to admire the fine stitching that held it together.

This was one of the few remaining copies of the first Indian Bible, printed in Cambridge in the year 1661, when Charles the Second was king of England. James's name does not appear in its pages. Yet, I knew that by this time, he was an apprentice to printer Samuel Green, whose name is on the title page. And James had worked on this Bible, its words in the Algonquian language that he spoke as well as the English he learned as a boy. He had helped to set the type, feed the paper into the press, and sew the separate sections together. I could feel his presence in the book as I turned it in my hands.

James Printer is mentioned in passing in many diaries and histories of King Philip's War, written at the time or soon after. It is from these sharp, little fragments that I have tried to reconstruct some sense of a long, rich life and explain how he came to join a rebellion against the English he had known all his life.

As boys, he and a cousin were taken into the house of Harvard's President Dunster, where there was a print shop. Later, the press was moved to what had been an Indian college next to the main college. The brick building was torn down in 1698. I like to think that occasional bits of lead type can be found even now in Harvard Yard, including a few that Sam Green might have thrown at his young half-brother Bartholomew.

During the war, James fled from Cambridge and was brought back along with several others by Captain Samuel Moseley. One Indian, called Little John, was sentenced to hang on the Boston Common, but was killed instead by another Indian who stabbed him in the chest. James was released a few days later, along with the other captives. He found his way to King Philip's camp, where he served as a scribe and translator and played an important role in the release of English hostages. He is also thought to be the author of the note left on the bridge at Medfield, warning the English that "the Indians thou has provoked in wrath and anger will war this twenty-one years if you will."

Like all wars, this uprising of Indians against the growing numbers of English immigrants was full of violence and the worst sort of atrocities on both sides. It was almost impossible to

remain neutral. James had to choose
he did.

Although he is listed in several his
early New England printers, James's
peared on only a single publication,
Experience Mayhew's 1709 book of p
English and in Algonquian. It is ther
title page, alongside the name of Bartl
Green, where it properly belongs.

— Paul Samue
July 1, 1996
Davis, Calif

moved to what had been an Indian college next to the main college. The brick building was torn down in 1698. I like to think that occasional bits of lead type can be found even now in Harvard Yard, including a few that Sam Green might have thrown at his young half-brother Bartholomew.

During the war, James fled from Cambridge and was brought back along with several others by Captain Samuel Moseley. One Indian, called Little John, was sentenced to hang on the Boston Common, but was killed instead by another Indian who stabbed him in the chest. James was released a few days later, along with the other captives. He found his way to King Philip's camp, where he served as a scribe and translator and played an important role in the release of English hostages. He is also thought to be the author of the note left on the bridge at Medfield, warning the English that "the Indians thou has provoked in wrath and anger will war this twenty-one years if you will."

Like all wars, this uprising of Indians against the growing numbers of English immigrants was full of violence and the worst sort of atrocities on both sides. It was almost impossible to remain neutral. James had to choose the side he did.

Although he is listed in several histories of early New England printers, James's name appeared on only a single publication, Master Experience Mayhew's 1709 book of psalms, in English and in Algonquian. It is there on the title page, alongside the name of Bartholomew Green, where it properly belongs.

— Paul Samuel Jacobs
July 1, 1996
Davis, California